W9-ABT-342

Dear Reader,

From February 2013 onward, Harlequin Romance will continue to offer four great reads every month, with all the themes you love, such as babies, weddings, bosses, pregnancies and more.

You can also find some of the authors you have come to know and love from Harlequin Romance in our new contemporary series Harlequin KISS, which is launching in February 2013.

Happy reading!

The Harlequin Romance Editors

P.S. Available this month:

#4357 THE HEIR'S PROPOSAL
Raye Morgan

#4358 THE SOLDIER'S SWEETHEART
The Larkville Legacy
Soraya Lane

#4359 THE BILLIONAIRE'S FAIR LADY
Barbara Wallace

#4360 A BRIDE FOR THE MAVERICK MILLIONAIRE
Journey Through the Outback
Marion Lennox

#4361 SHIPWRECKED WITH MR. WRONG
Nikki Logan

#4362 WHEN CHOCOLATE IS NOT ENOUGH…
Nina Harrington

Praise for Raye Morgan

"Morgan's latest is a delightful reworking of a classic plot, with well-drawn characters—particularly tortured hero Max—and just the right amount of humor to offset his tragic past."
—*RT Book Reviews* on
Beauty and the Reclusive Prince

"This is a fun story with interesting characters. Despite the fantasy setting, Morgan brings a serious twist to the story as Kayla and Max deal with painful events in their past."
—*RT Book Reviews* on
Taming the Lost Prince

RAYE MORGAN

The Heir's Proposal

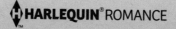

If you purchased this book without a cover you should be aware
that this book is stolen property. It was reported as "unsold and
destroyed" to the publisher, and neither the author nor the
publisher has received any payment for this "stripped book."

Recycling programs
for this product may
not exist in your area.

ISBN-13: 978-0-373-74222-6

THE HEIR'S PROPOSAL

First North American Publication 2013

Copyright © 2013 by Helen Conrad

All rights reserved. Except for use in any review, the reproduction or
utilization of this work in whole or in part in any form by any electronic,
mechanical or other means, now known or hereafter invented, including
xerography, photocopying and recording, or in any information storage
or retrieval system, is forbidden without the written permission of the
publisher, Harlequin Enterprises Limited, 225 Duncan Mill Road,
Don Mills, Ontario M3B 3K9, Canada.

This is a work of fiction. Names, characters, places and incidents are
either the product of the author's imagination or are used fictitiously,
and any resemblance to actual persons, living or dead, business
establishments, events or locales is entirely coincidental.

This edition published by arrangement with Harlequin Books S.A.

For questions and comments about the quality of this book,
please contact us at CustomerService@Harlequin.com.

® and TM are trademarks of Harlequin Enterprises Limited or its
corporate affiliates. Trademarks indicated with ® are registered in the
United States Patent and Trademark Office, the Canadian Trade Marks
Office and in other countries.

HARLEQUIN®
www.Harlequin.com

Printed in U.S.A.

Raye Morgan has been a nursery school teacher, a travel agent, a clerk and a business editor, but her best job ever has been writing romances—and fostering romance in her own family at the same time. Current score: two boys married, two more to go. Raye has published more than seventy romance novels, and claims to have many more waiting in the wings. She lives in Southern California, with her husband and whichever son happens to be staying at home at the moment.

Books by Raye Morgan

Other titles by this author available in ebook format.

This story is dedicated to Bets in Santa Fe.

CHAPTER ONE

TORIE Sands was shivering so hard her teeth clattered together. Not only was she cold, she was—well, sort of scared.

What in the world was she going to do? She'd come out onto this spit of land when the sun was still shining, California-beach style, and she'd gone on a sentimental journey around the rock, looking for her childhood in the caves. She'd forgotten how quickly the weather could change out here—not to mention the water level.

Now she was stuck. The spit turned into an island at high tide. And the fog had come in—not on little cat feet, but like a wild herd of ghostly mustangs, silent and deadly, sweeping in with a vengeance.

She remembered now. This sort of thing was called a killer fog when she was a kid and living up on the cliff above, the only child of the Huntington family butler. She knew she should be able to swim or wade to the shore, but she couldn't see land and the current was running hard toward the open sea. If she got caught up in that…

A crack of thunder made her jump. Great. Now it was probably going to rain.

How was she going to get out of here? She hadn't told anyone where she was going. Her cell phone was telling her No Service. She hadn't brought along any flares. Could she possibly spend the night out here? No!

And then she was eaten by the slimy sea monster…

The phrase came sailing into her head from some long-forgotten campfire story from her childhood. Ah, memories. She shivered that much harder.

Okay, time to call for help. She hadn't seen another soul as she'd come sashaying down through the dunes and across the wet sand bridge, but just in case… After all, what other option did she have?

"Help!" she yelled as loudly as she could. "Help! I'm caught out here on the island. Help!"

Nothing. Just the sound of water slapping against the shore in rhythmic waves. In the distance—the far, far distance—she could hear the lonely call of a foghorn. She pulled her arms in close and winced as the wind slapped her hair into her eyes. This was no fun and she was bordering on hysteria.

"Mrs. Marino?" A deep male voice came arcing through the gloom. "Are you out there?"

She gasped with relief. Human contact! Maybe she wasn't going to die out here in the cold after all.

It took her a moment to register the name, though.

Mrs. Marino? What? Oh. That was the name she was going under so as not to alert the Huntingtons as to who she really was. She shouldn't give out any hints that it was a phony.

"Yes," she called back, surprised to hear how her voice quavered. "I'm here. What should I do? How do I get back to the other side?"

"Just hold on. I'm coming to get you."

She took a deep breath and closed her eyes for a moment. She was already in love with that voice. He sounded hard and male and sure of himself. *Confidence.* That was the key word here. Hopefully, the man would fit the voice and she would be safe. Hopefully.

* * *

Marc Huntington was growling softly as he began to pull off his jacket and then his long-sleeved knit shirt. This was not exactly the way he'd planned to spend his afternoon—rescuing one of the vultures who had come to Shangri-La, his family estate, to pick the bones clean.

He knew the situation. There was no money left. He'd come back home just in time to watch his heritage be destroyed. Unfortunately, his ten years in the military hadn't equipped him with the kind of funds needed to pay the back taxes his mother had ignored for too long. Selling the entire estate seemed to her to be the only way to deal with the problem and she was the official owner. It was her call.

So Shangri-La was up for sale. His mother's elaborate advertisements had produced a set of eight visitors here for the weekend, here to look the place over and come up with their offers. Every one of them was a grifter as far as he could tell. He could have cheerfully watched them all drown.

Well, not actually. His years as a Navy SEAL had ingrained the protective, rescuing ethic in his mind so thoroughly, it would take more than pure loathing to cleanse it from his soul. It was a part of him. How did you un-learn something like that?

"Talk to me," he ordered the stranded lady he couldn't see. "As I go through the current, it'll help keep me on course."

"Okay," she called back, sounding less scared now. "What shall I talk about?"

He was growling again. What did it matter what she talked about? He wasn't going to listen to anything but the sound of her voice. Her actual words weren't important. Maybe he should tell her to recite the details of the terms she was planning to offer in buying out his family estate. Hah.

"Sing a song," he suggested, looking down at his board shorts and deciding not to strip quite that far. He'd taken off the shirt and jacket because he might have to swim if the water was deep enough. But going down to his boxers wouldn't help much. "Recite a poem. Whatever."

He stepped into the icy water, feeling it wash against his legs even though the fog was so thick, he could barely see anything. Across the way, he could hear the woman beginning to sing something. She had a nice voice. He stopped and listened. Whatever that was she was singing, it had a familiar sound to it, like a Celtic folk song. Where had he heard that before?

He shook his head. It didn't matter. If she could keep it up, he would find her soon enough. One last growl and he plunged into the current, heading for the high, clear voice he heard through the fog.

Torie heard him coming through the water. He was getting closer. Sweet gratitude surged through her system. She raised her face to where the sun should be and sang harder and higher, trying to give him a clear signal as to her location.

And then she heard splashing very close and in a minute or two she began to make out the dark shape of a man coming toward her.

"Oh, thank God," she cried as he approached. "I was afraid I was going to have to spend the night out here in the cold."

He didn't speak and as he came closer, she could make out his features and she began to realize he had a familiar look to him. She frowned. Oh no! It couldn't be.

He stopped a couple of feet away. "Mrs. Marino, I'm Marc Huntington. Marge is my mother. Just so you know I' m not some random beach bum."

Her heart began to thud in her chest. Marc Huntington. What was he doing here? It had been years since she'd seen him—at least fifteen of them. She'd heard he was overseas, in the service, fighting bad guys and raising hell.

But here he was, staring at her and looking none too friendly, despite his polite words. "How did you get out here, anyway?" he growled. "And why?"

He didn't recognize her. That was a relief. But why should he? She barely recognized him—and wouldn't have if she'd met up with him anywhere else. The last time she'd seen him, he'd been about half this size, a lanky, smart-mouthed teenager who probably didn't even know she existed.

Now he was all corded chest muscles and wide shoulders, with dark hair that tended to fall over his forehead and crystal-blue eyes that seemed remarkably hostile. Bottom line—he was pretty much the most gorgeous man she'd ever seen. She drew her breath in sharply and couldn't say a word.

His brow furrowed. "Are you okay?"

She nodded. It took two tries before she could speak. "Uh…I'm…my name is Torie… But I guess you know that. I was just exploring the caves and the fog came in and… and…"

"Okay," he said impatiently. "No problem. Your husband was getting excited when you didn't show up for tea. Everyone is out looking for you."

Husband? Husband? She didn't have a husband. Oh. But she did have Carl Marino, and he was pretending to be her husband. She had to keep that straight in her mind.

"I'm sorry to be a bother," she said, finally getting control of herself. The shock of coming face to face with the man version of the boy she'd had a crush on for years had thrown her for a loop, but she was getting her balance back. She had to remember he was the enemy, just like everyone else in the Huntington family—the enemy she'd come to slay like a proverbial dragon.

And now here was one of them, saving her from the cold. A bit awkward, to say the least.

"I lost track of time."

He nodded, his blue-eyed gaze skimming over her bare arms and legs in the skimpy sundress she'd worn. "Next time, bring a jacket," he suggested gruffly. "It can turn cold fast."

And she'd known that. After all, she'd spent every summer of her childhood right here on this very beach. But it had been a good fifteen years since her last visit and she'd been so excited to see her old secret places, she'd forgotten about the vagaries of the weather.

"I'm okay," she insisted, despite her chattering teeth. "Are you going to lead me back?"

He looked her up and down and, for the first time, there was a hint of humor in his eyes.

"No," he said. "I'm going to carry you."

"What?" She began to back away from him on the sand. "No. You can't carry me all the way back."

"Why not? I'm trained to carry awkward loads, and you definitely look like a lightweight anyway."

She stopped and glared at him. Was he making fun of her? Why the hostility when he thought he'd only just met her?

"Awkward and bird-brained at the same time?" she asked crisply. "I didn't realize you knew me that well."

His mouth twisted. "That isn't what I meant."

"No, but it's what you said."

His look was long-suffering. "Mrs. Marino, your husband is having a fit back at the house. He seems to think you're likely to walk off a cliff or something, unless you're carefully watched. So I intend to make sure you get back safely." He made a gesture with his head. "Come on. Let's get this over with."

She looked at him, at the smooth, hard flesh she was going to have to touch in order to do what he'd suggested, and her heart began to pound like a hammer. There was a time when she'd dreamed about touching him—but that was when she was half in love with him from afar. Now, the thought was horrifying. He was the enemy. She couldn't do it.

"No," she said. "I'll follow you. I'll…I'll hold on to…" She was going to say, *your shirt,* but he wasn't wearing one, and the only alternative was the back of his low-slung board shorts. The thought of sticking her fingers down there made her gasp.

He watched her, waiting as her face registered a growing realization of the problem.

"Exactly," he said, his voice mocking. "I'll carry you," he said again.

She was shaking her head. "I don't think so."

His patience was running thin and it showed. "Listen carefully. There is a hard current running through the deepest part of the channel, right where we have to cross. If it knocks you down, the strength of it could carry you right out to sea. Then I would have to swim out after you, and I don't know how successful I'd be. It's safer for all concerned if you just let me pick you up and …"

"Isn't there some other way?"

His frown was getting fiercer. "What is your problem?"

She drew in a deep breath and told him with a glare. "You're almost naked, you know."

He gave her a look that said he thought she was nuts. "You're not exactly well-covered yourself. If we'd been swimming, you wouldn't think twice."

"But…"

"Look, every minute we delay, it's only getting worse. Come on." His quick smile was sarcastic. "I'll be gentle, I swear it."

By now she was seriously annoyed with him. He wasn't even trying to see this from her point of view—and he had no interest in exploring alternatives. She looked around, trying to think of some way to avoid this, and he took a step forward and grabbed her, swinging her up into his arms. It was pretty obvious he wouldn't mind just chucking her over his shoulder, good to go, but when she shrieked he relented and straightened her so that one arm was under her knees and the other behind her back. She threw her arms around his neck to avoid being dropped, and they started off.

He was impossibly hard and exciting to touch, but even worse, his incredible warmth worked on her like a drug. She was clinging to him, trying to get closer. She closed her eyes and took it all in, trying to pretend he wasn't the boy she used to watch with stars in her eyes.

Those stars had dimmed when the Huntingtons had fired her father, accused him of crimes and kicked her whole family out of what had long been their beloved home. Let's face it, the Huntingtons had pretty much destroyed her family and torn apart their lives—and all over a lie. Nothing had ever been the same again and the pain and resentment still smoldered deep inside her.

But she'd never been in stronger arms. It felt good—as long as she didn't think about who he really was.

The water was surging against him and she could feel the effort it took him to keep his footing. He almost went over at one point, splashing a spray of seawater against her legs, and she cried out, holding on more tightly, pressing her face against his neck.

"I've got you," he told her gruffly. "Just a little bit more. We're almost there."

She peeked out. She couldn't see a thing but the cold, clammy gray of the fog. How did he know they were almost there? She couldn't tell. But she knew one thing—his skin against hers felt like heaven. To think she'd been resisting.

But the fog was lifting and she began to see the shore herself.

"Here we are," he said, and she could feel the difference in the way he was walking. They'd hit dry sand. He began to lower her and she felt a pang of regret.

"Put on my jacket," he told her as he picked it up off the sand and handed it to her. She did as he suggested. It was big and heavy, made of denim with a few studs at the pockets— and it still felt warm, as though his body heat had lasted.

She turned to look at him. His arms were raised and he was pulling a long-sleeved thermal shirt down over his head. She watched, marveling at the interplay of muscles, and then gasped as she noticed the deep, ugly scar that disfigured an area of his rib cage.

Her shocked gaze met his ice-blue eyes as the shirt came down into place and covered everything—the muscles and the scar. She blinked at him, feeling breathless.

She wanted to ask about the scar, but the look in his eyes told her not to do it. Still, she had to say something. It was only right.

"Did you do something horribly brave that saved the day?" she asked a bit too quickly.

His look was dismissive. "No. I did something horribly stupid and ended up injured, which is something you never want to let happen."

"Oh. Of course."

But she didn't want him to think she was just a snotty brat. She needed to let him know she did appreciate what he'd done for her.

"Thank you," she said at last, feeling almost shy now that they were on firm ground and about to end their rescue encounter. "I really appreciate it. I mean…"

"What I'd appreciate," he said, his voice calm but icy, "is some answers."

She'd been stopped in the middle of her sentence, and she was still staring at him. "Uh… answers? About what?"

"About what you're doing here. Why you came."

She blinked at him, a flicker of panic near her heart. Had he really caught on to her so quickly? "I...we came to see the estate, of course. It's for sale, isn't it?"

He nodded, waiting.

"Well, we came to see if Carl wants...I mean if we want to buy it. Isn't that what this is all about?"

His gaze never left her eyes. "You'd think. That's what all eight of you people came for, to spend the weekend looking over the property, evaluating it." His eyes narrowed. "I would have thought the house itself would be the main attraction. Either that, or the patio, the waterfall area, the huge front yard. And yet you'd hardly dropped your bags in the bedroom before you were off to see the caves. And your husband was off to nose around in the old vineyard area." He cocked an eyebrow. "What gives?"

She frowned at him. She hadn't realized Carl had gone off on his own sightseeing mission. She had to admit, it might look odd that the two of them had been so driven by alternate goals so immediately. She ought to do her best to quell all suspicions—if she could.

"What do you mean, 'what gives?' Nothing. We're just interested in everything, the house, the land, the beaches. I'd heard about the caves and…and I wanted to see them for myself."

He didn't look convinced. "The caves are cool, but they're hardly the best feature on the estate." He eyed her speculatively. "They do have a lot of historical significance," he said. "Smugglers seem to like them, and have since the old Spanish days." His gaze narrowed and he added acidly, "Is that what you were doing out there? Hiding something?"

She wanted to laugh out loud at such a silly suggestion, but she could see that this was no joke in his mind. "If I were, I wouldn't tell you about it, would I?" She bit her lip, regretting her words before she'd finished uttering them.

Keep it friendly, Torie, she told herself silently. *Save the anger for when you've got the ammunition.*

She quickly added out loud, "I'm going to enjoy seeing everything. It seems to be a wonderful property."

"Oh, it is that." A stormy look filled his blue eyes. "And it's worth a whole lot more than my mother is asking for it." He gave her a faint, sarcastic smile. "But you know that, don't you?"

A crash of thunder seemed to give an eerie

emphasis to his words and large raindrops began spattering around them. Torie was shivering again.

CHAPTER TWO

THUNDER rolled and the rain began in earnest. Looking up, Marc swore under his breath.

"The fog no sooner thins out than the rain comes," he grumbled. "Come on. We'll never make it back across the dunes. Head for the tool shed just beyond the ice plant over there."

He pointed toward a wooden structure only a few hundred feet away and they ran for it, reaching it in moments, the threat of a downpour chasing them. Luckily the door wasn't locked and they tumbled in, breathing hard and laughing. Marc slammed the door shut, holding back the cold, wet wind, then turned to look at her.

They were both still laughing from the run across the sand, but Torie saw the humor fade in his eyes, and she looked away quickly.

"This shouldn't last too long," he said. "We might as well have a seat and wait it out."

The interior of the shed seemed clean

enough, with tools piled along one side and bags of gravel and peat moss stacked along the other. They sat down on the plastic bags and listened to the rain pound on the roof. A couple of leaks appeared along the walls, but they weren't bad. Neither of them spoke, and the rain was too loud to try to talk over anyway.

Marc's head was turned away, looking out a small window at the rain, and Torie had time to study him, the back of his head and the angle of his neck and the width of his shoulders.

She shivered again, but not with cold. She was beginning to realize this wasn't going to be easy. How could she ever have imagined it might be? For fifteen years, she'd hated the Huntingtons. They'd seemed like monsters in her mind. She'd ached to find a way to clear her father's name and turn the world right again.

But now that she'd come face to face with them, things looked a bit different. If she'd succeed, she needed to be smart about it. She was going to have to stay strong. Reality had a way of cancelling out fantasy every time.

They were just people. That didn't mean they weren't guilty of some ugly things. But they were still proving to be only human— for now.

First there had been Marge, Marc's mother. When she and Carl had come up the front walk and climbed the steps to the wide porch and the huge front door, her heart had been pounding so hard, she'd thought she might faint. And then the door had swung open and there was this short, redheaded woman in a simple pants suit, welcoming them to Shangri-La with a warm smile. She didn't look much like the Cruella de Vil monster Torie had been remembering her as all these years. In fact, she looked more like a Brownie den mother. Sort of a letdown.

Marc's older sister Shayla had shown them to their rooms. She was a little closer to the mark. She'd always been snooty and full of herself, and things hadn't changed. But Torie had to admit, even she didn't seem like a fiend close up.

There had been two boys in the family, Marc and his older brother Ricky. Torie had assumed, as she and Carl had first arrived, that both young men were off living their own lives somewhere by now. The surprise had been to find Marc here.

Of course, the one most to blame for what happened, Marc's father, Tim Huntington, usually called Hunt, wasn't here at all. He'd drowned when his sailboat capsized in the bay years before. She would never be able to confront him. There would always be a hole in her soul for that.

In her dreams, she came charging up to Shangri-La and found the evidence to clear her father, presented it to Marge and Shayla with a flourish, and had them dissolving into tears of regret and apology. She would demand they write up a complete retraction and send it to the *Alegre Beacon*, the local paper. The little town of Alegre would be thrown into an uproar. The mayor would name a special celebration and present Torie with a plaque commemorating the day.

And Torie would take the plaque back down to Los Angeles and present it to her mother. That was her dream.

At least, it had been for years. She'd recently discovered evidence that cast a shadow on those hopes. Was there more to all this than she'd ever known? Possibly. And that was the main reason she was here today.

The downpour was almost over. The noise on the roof had faded to a dull drumbeat. Marc turned and looked at her, his blue eyes full of skepticism.

"So tell me about Carl," he said without preamble.

Her eyes widened. She hadn't really expected that. "What about him?"

"How long have you and Carl been married?" he asked her.

She frowned. She hated questions like this. She really didn't want to lie. But what could she do? Try to avoid it, she supposed. Just dance around the facts any way she could.

"Not long," she said brightly.

"Newlyweds, huh?"

She gave him a vague smile. She couldn't imagine Carl as a newlywed—not to anyone. He was a fairly cold, unemotional person. Business deals were all he cared about. Her accompanying him here was all part of a bargain to him. He needed to pretend to have a wife—she needed a way to get onto Shangri-La without letting the Huntingtons know who she was. They'd struck a deal.

"Any kids?"

"No. Oh no."

"I guess not if you always ask for separate bedrooms."

She flushed and her eyes flashed, but she held her temper. "Carl snores," she said, reciting the excuse they'd given when they made their reservations. That had been her one demand when Carl had asked her to come along. It had to be separate bedrooms, no matter how strange that looked.

Marc's eyes narrowed. "Carl's a bit older than you are, isn't he?"

She wasn't going to dignify that with an answer. Suddenly the bag of gravel felt hard and uncomfortable, and she got up to stretch her legs a bit. There wasn't much room for pacing, but she did her best.

"Where did you two meet?"

She glanced at him. The question flustered her. Her fingers were trembling. He was going to figure this whole charade out, wasn't he? He wanted to catch hold of a string and begin to pull it all apart. She could see it coming. But she had to make an attempt—keep her finger in the dike, so to speak.

"I...uh...he hired me to plan some cocktail parties for his business clients."

"You're a party planner?"

"And a caterer." She nodded, brightening to a theme she knew well and something she didn't have to skate around. "Yes. Any event, large or small. I can make it magical."

"I'll bet you can." His smile was ironic. "So you partied and you fell in love?"

She frowned, not trusting him at all. "You might say that."

Okay, it was time she got a little tougher. She couldn't let him think he had the upper hand. Turning, she glared at him.

"Listen, Marc. What's with the third degree? What is this intense interest in my private life?"

His wide mouth twisted. Maybe he was coming on a bit too strong.

There was no doubt he was suspicious—suspicious of every one of the visitors they were stuck with for the weekend. The last time they'd had an influx of strangers like this had been shortly after his father had died, drowned just outside the bay when his small sailboat had capsized. Once the word had spread that he'd taken the Don Carlos Treasure down with him, fortune hunters had come crawling all over the place. None of them believed that the old Spanish fortune that had been in the Huntington family for over a hundred years had really gone down into the sea. Everyone thought if he just looked hard enough, he would find the hiding place.

And the place searched most often were the caves. Of course. The caves had been where the treasure was first found. And the caves had been where the treasure had been hidden the first time it had disappeared.

But not this last time. Experts had gone over the place with a fine-tooth comb. There was no treasure, not anymore. It was pretty obvious his father's suicide note had said it all. The Don Carlos Treasure had gone back to the sea, from whence it had come.

Ashes to ashes, dust to dust and Spanish doubloons back to Neptune.

So was that what this pretty young woman had been looking for in the caves? Of course it was. Why else would she hurry right out there? She even had the look of a treasure hunter—always hopeful.

His gaze held hers for a long moment. There was a spark of humor in his eyes, but that didn't make her feel any better about this air of tension between them. Finally, he actually smiled.

"No big deal," he said. "Just making conversation. Passing the time." He slid off his bag as well and faced her in the small space. "I think the rain has stopped. Let's go."

She took a deep breath and watched as he left the shed, then hurried to catch up with him. He started across the dunes, striding quickly in the wet sand, and she had to run to keep up. His legs were much longer than hers.

About halfway to the cliff, he stopped, turning to watch her arrive at his position.

"Rest a minute," he said.

"I wouldn't need to if you wouldn't go so fast," she said testily.

"Sorry." But his gaze was restless. He looked toward the large white house up on the cliff. "I can't help but wonder what they're doing up there," he said, mostly to himself. He shook his head. "What is she thinking?"

"Who?" Torie asked, though she was pretty sure he meant Marge. "What's wrong?"

"*Turning and turning,*" he muttered, along with some other words she couldn't make out. He was staring into the distance. "*The center cannot hold.*"

"What?"

He looked directly into her eyes. "I think I'm in need of some 'passionate intensity'," he said.

Funny, but those words seemed to strike a chord with her. "Me too," she said. "Where do I go to get some?"

His grin was quick and then gone just as quickly. "Try a little Yeats," he suggested. "That just might be your answer."

And he was off again across the sands.

She came behind him, muttering about Lawrence of Arabia, but he didn't go as quickly this time and she arrived at the end of their mad scramble across the dunes only seconds after he did.

"My dear Mrs. Marino." He said with a touch of sarcasm. "We have reached the end of the line. I think we'd better part company here."

"You're not going up to the house?"

"Not yet. I have things to do in another part of the estate."

"Oh. Well, I guess I'll see you later."

"Unfortunately, I think you're right."

He sounded bitter, but before she had a chance to analyze that, he stepped closer and grabbed the two sides of the jacket, acting as though he was straightening the collar, but she was pretty sure he was really just trying to make a point—and maybe trying to establish his sense of control. The way he pulled on the jacket, she had to look up into his face.

"I still want to know what the hell you were doing in the caves," he said, his voice low and harsh. "You want to come clean now, or wait until I've got more information to go on?"

She stared up at him, shaken. His face was

only inches from hers. "Uh…nothing. I was just exploring. I…I love the beach and I…"

But an expression flashed across his face and suddenly he was frowning, studying her features, his gaze sliding over every angle.

"Do I know you?" he asked softly.

Her heart was thumping so hard surely he could hear it. "I don't think so," she said quickly. "Now if you don't mind…."

"But I do mind." He pulled harder, bringing her up to where she could feel his warm breath on her face as he spoke. "And I'll give you fair warning. I won't let Shangri-La be trashed. Any excuse I can find to disqualify any of you, I'll use it."

She stared up, mesmerized by his voice and his eyes.

A shout from the cliff area turned them both in that direction. Carl was coming down the wooden steps.

"Torie!" he called. "Thank God you're okay."

She looked at Marc. He stared back, not letting go of the jacket. For a long moment, their gazes held. There was a look deep in his eyes, a mood, something that told her he was a bit of a loner, that he couldn't trust anyone enough to let go. Her heart seemed to melt, something in her yearned toward him. Someone ought to teach him how to trust. Too bad she was exactly the wrong person to expect that from.

She was the one who'd been lying to him all along. When he found out, he would discard her like yesterday's news.

But Carl was coming and it was obviously time to draw apart.

"Just keep that in mind, Mrs. Marino," Marc said coolly. "I'll be watching you."

He gave her one last impenetrably hard look, then turned and walked away.

Torie groaned as she watched him go. Marc Huntington would be watching her. Great. Maybe this was turnabout for the way she used to watch him when she was fifteen. She had to bite her lip to keep from laughing a bit hysterically, and she turned just as Carl reached her.

Tall and slim with thick auburn hair, Carl was handsome in an older way, and came across as very sure of himself. But right now, the man looked nervous.

Maybe Marc had threatened to watch him, too.

"What are you doing?" Carl whispered loudly, glancing toward where Marc was disappearing through the brush. "You're going to ruin the whole thing if you start messing around with young guys."

Messing around?

She drew back, offended. "He just saved me," she told him tartly. "I was in danger. Sort of."

"Where were you?" Carl asked, looking perplexed.

"Where were *you*?" she countered, pulling the jacket close around herself. "I heard you were out looking at the vineyard. I thought it was the house you were interested in."

His gaze shifted in a way that startled her. Was that a guilty look? He grabbed her arm and started leading her toward the stairs, muttering as he went.

He was annoyed but not really angry. She knew he didn't really care anything about her personally, he just didn't want anyone to get suspicious. And when you came right down to it, she felt the same way about him. The two of them were more like partners in this enterprise than anything else. They were definitely not a couple.

Carl looked back over his shoulder as they started up the wooden stairway. "Stay away from that guy," he said. "I can tell he's nothing but trouble."

"His name is Marc Huntington," she told him, in case he didn't know. "He's Marge Huntington's son."

"He didn't recognize you, did he?" he asked in alarm. He knew all about her childhood here in Shangri-La.

"No. I don't think so."

"Good."

She eyed him curiously. "I would think you might want to get friendly with him, not avoid him," she said. "He would probably be a good source of information about the property. And maybe have a little different perspective than his mother has." And then she remembered what he'd said just before Carl arrived. Maybe there was really no point in getting closer to Marc. Maybe it would be safer all around if Carl kept his distance.

Carl shrugged. "I think I can gain more by exploring the place on my own," he said, giving her a pointed look. "And that is something you are going to help me with."

"I am?"

He nodded. "Sure. What do you think I brought you for? You grew up on the place. You know all the secrets." He gave her a crafty smile. "Don't you, darling?"

They'd reached the wide front porch and

Marge Huntington was holding the door open for them, clucking over how everyone had been worried about Torie, freeing her from having to answer Carl's surprising statement. But she couldn't stop thinking about it. As she went up the stairs to dress for dinner, his words echoed in her mind.

You know all the secrets.

Something in his words chilled her. Maybe it was time she faced a few facts. She'd ignored her own doubts about Carl because he was giving her a chance to come back to Shangri-La, a chance she'd never have had without him. He'd told her he wanted her along to give the impression he was a stable married man, to help his chances of buying the place.

But now that they were here, she was beginning to realize there was more to it. When he'd quizzed her about her life her as a kid, she'd been happy to spill out just about everything she could think of. The trip down memory lane had been worth it. But now his interest seemed more pointed, less general. What was he after, anyway? That started her shivering again, despite the warmth of Marc's jacket.

The room she'd been given was a little

heavy on the pink accents for her taste, but it was certainly charming. There was an old-fashioned canopy over the bed and plush, heart-shaped cushions everywhere. There were two doors besides the entryway—one to the private balcony and the other to the bathroom.

She shrugged out of Marc's jacket and threw it over the back of a chair, then walked out onto the little balcony and leaned out over the white wooden railing with its Victorian ornamentation. She could just barely make out the red tile roof of the butler's cottage where she'd lived as a child. Just seeing it brought a lump to her throat.

"I'm back, Huntingtons," she whispered to herself. "I'm back and I'm going to find out what really happened fifteen years ago when you fired my father and destroyed my family." She flipped her thick blond hair back with a toss of her head. "Get ready for it. I want some answers, too."

Shangri-La.

The name conjured up images of the mysterious East, and yet, the Huntington estate was plunked right in the middle of the California central coast and looked it. The house was a huge old rambling Victorian, perched on a cliff over the ocean, and there was nothing mysterious about it.

Torie did a little exploring, disappointed to find the grounds had been changed here and there. The beautiful rose garden that Mr. Huntington had been so proud of was a barren mess, and the trellis along the ocean cliff was gone. A new set of buildings lined the driveway and a new pool complex filled what had once been the tennis court area. The changes gave her a sick, empty feeling and she went back into the house, slipping quietly down the hallways to get a feel for the place.

She found the kitchen, and just as she turned to go again, Marc appeared in the doorway.

"Looking for something?" he asked, gazing at her skeptically.

She blinked, feeling guilty for no reason at all. "Just a drink of water."

He went to the cabinet and got down a glass, then poured her a drink from the pitcher next to the sink. Turning, he watched her levelly as she drank it down.

"Shouldn't you be attending to your husband?" he said, his voice soft but filled with a sense of irony.

"My...?"

Funny. Whenever Marc came near, she completely forgot that she was pretending to be married to someone.

"Uh, no," she said quickly, using a phony smile as a cover-up. "Carl is actually pretty self-sufficient."

"Lucky you," he noted, his gaze cool.

She smiled at him but he didn't smile back and she retreated quickly, pulse beating a bit too fast. This might be Shangri-La, but it wasn't paradise. Too many conflicting emotions for that.

Another name came to mind as Torie sat at the dinner table, looking at the eclectic gallery of other perspective buyers. Actually, she was reminded of the cantina scene in the original *Star Wars*. A den of villainy, no doubt about it. Not to mention strangeness.

There was Tom, the jovial Texan whose booming laugh filled the room and bounced from the walls. Sitting next to him was the stylishly dressed Lyla, a pretty young widow from Los Angeles, who looked upon them all with a sense of disdain flaring her elegant nostrils. Andros, a Greek restaurateur, and his wife Nina, seemed pleasant and friendly, but Phoebe, the voluptuous blonde in the low-cut dress, and Frank, the vaguely sinister-looking real estate broker who dressed as though he was trying out for a role in a local production of *Saturday Night Fever*, were a couple she wouldn't have wanted to meet in an alley on a dark night.

Marge Huntington presided at the head of the table, attempting to tame them all with pleasantries and offers to pass the au jus. She hardly looked any older than she had fifteen years ago, her flaming red hair flying like a flag. Torie remembered seeing her out sunbathing on the beach and hosting luncheons for the local women's groups.

She'd been jumpy at first, wondering if the woman would remember her, but Marge hadn't given her a second glance. She didn't recognize her—and why should she? Her name had been Vikki then, short for Victoria, and she'd been short and chubby, with mousy brown hair and no personality that she could remember having. A typical plain Jane sort of girl, short on friends and scared of her own shadow.

That was then. This was now. She'd learned a thing or two about making herself ready for her place on the stage of life. She was taller, thinner, blonder—and definitely more confident.

Even so, sitting at the table with the woman made Torie a little nervous. Every time her eyes met Marge's, she felt a little surge in her heart rate. She couldn't help but think her hostess was going to begin to recognize her at some point.

But maybe that wouldn't happen. After all, Marge was pretty self-absorbed. As long as she was the center of attention, she didn't seem to need anything else.

She'd been prepared to face Marge, but it had never occurred to her that Marc might be here. She wondered if that was going to be the fatal flaw. Marc could very possibly ruin all her plans.

The food was good—cold trout and roasted Cornish game hens with a warm caramel apple pie for dessert. She noticed that the butler, a semi-handsome young man whom they called Jimmy in an annoyingly casual manner, was exchanging the sort of looks with Marge that usually meant bedroom visits late at night—but she didn't care. She was just glad her father wasn't here to see the Shangri-La butler being so unprofessional. He would have been appalled.

Marge welcomed them all and laid out the plans for the weekend.

"I want you to love Shangri-La like we do," she said, smiling at each in turn around the table. "I want you to feel what it's like to have the ocean in your front yard. I want you to explore the gardens, the vineyards, the cliffs. I want you to ride into town and visit our quaint little stores. Once you get a true feeling for the place, for the possibilities, I know you'll see how it could change and enrich your life."

The Texan gave a grunt of amusement. "And then you're hoping one of us will be ready to 'change and enrich' yours with a nice ownership bid, aren't you?"

Marge didn't flinch. "Of course. That's the whole point, isn't it?"

Everyone laughed, but a bit tentatively, glancing sideways at each other. After all, if they did all love the estate, they would all soon be fighting each other for the chance to own it.

Lyla began going on and on about the invigorating effects of fresh sea air while Phoebe was throwing flirtatious glances at the Texan. Torie looked at Carl sitting next to her and found that he was staring at his food as though his mind was off in some other place.

And then an odd thing happened. The hair on the back of her neck was rising. She glanced up quickly and found Marc leaning against the doorjamb, arms folded across his chest, watching her coolly. He was wearing a long-sleeved jersey shirt that said Airborne just above where his forearms sat. He had the look of a man who was deciding who was naughty and who was nice. She was afraid she could already tell which category he had her in.

Funny. A look like that from Marc Huntington would have sent her running for a hiding place in the old days. But times had changed. She was all grown up and had a temper of her own. So she raised her wineglass as though toasting him and smiled.

His face didn't change but something glittered in his eyes. Was that a hint of humor? Couldn't be—not in a tough guy like Marc. She shrugged, raised her chin and put the glass down. He was obviously in fight mode, just searching for ways to stop his mother's plans. She actually had no interest in either side of that struggle. She had her own agenda.

Marc stayed where he was and studied each one of the characters around his family dining table in turn. Every one of them seemed have hidden motives. Every one of them needed to be watched.

Or was he just being paranoid? Too many months on the front lines of war tended to do that to a man. He had to watch out. He'd known others from his line of work who ended up raving against reality, seeing assassins behind every tree. He didn't want to be like that.

His biggest problem right now was that his gaze kept getting tugged back to Torie. Wasn't there a phrase for that? He couldn't keep his eyes off her. That was it.

There was no getting around it—something about her appealed to him in a core, involuntary way. It was visceral. It came from inside him and he couldn't get it to stop.

He didn't trust her and he certainly didn't trust Carl. He'd already put in a call to an old friend in local law enforcement who sometimes worked with the FBI to see if he could find out something about Carl. The man just had a gangland look about him. What in hell a woman like Torie was doing with scum like that, he couldn't imagine. He didn't want to believe what that pointed to—that she was just as bad as he was. Or at least, willing to tolerate his badness.

But never mind. It wasn't as if he was falling for her or anything. It had been a long time since a woman had really yanked his chain and he thought he'd been pretty much inoculated against it.

He was a Navy SEAL for God's sake. He'd been out and seen the world and the world had done it's damndest to him. He'd been shot at, he'd been attacked by a man with a knife and a deadly grudge, he'd been in bar fights. He'd been loved by some beautiful women and hated by others. He'd lived, and he planned to live some more.

But what he hadn't planned for were the feelings, the emotions, that coming home had delivered like a blow to the gut. Coming back to Shangri-La, seeing its majestic beauty again, remembering his life, his father, his brother, and all that they had meant to each other—those emotions had surged through him and pierced his heart, cutting to the soul of who he was and where he came from.

His gaze kept shifting back toward Torie. He liked the look of her. There was love and laughter in that face, and a lively intelligence. Most women he'd known had one or another of those qualities. But she seemed to have them all in spades.

But there was something else that teased his imagination. Every now and then when he looked at her, he caught an expression in her eyes that he couldn't quite analyze. Was it sadness? Regret? Or fear? She was always quick to erase it with a smile and he hadn't had time to get a fix on it yet.

But he knew one thing about her for sure— she wasn't in love with Carl. That was clear. She might be in love with someone, but this guy wasn't it. A little part of him felt a twinge of jealousy.

He grimaced. Ridiculous. He could admit she attracted him, but even that was off limits. She was married, and even if she didn't love Carl, that was a situation he would stay a million miles away from.

At the same time, he didn't trust her. How could he? She lied every time she spoke to him. Why didn't he hate her for it?

No. He couldn't hate her. Even her lying was cute, like a kitten who couldn't help but bite you.

Whoa. He seemed to be about to hand her carte blanche for anything. This was ridiculously dangerous. He had to get out of this mood and fast.

He shifted his gaze to his mother. Except,

she wasn't really his mother. It had been drummed into his head that he had to call her that, but it had never penetrated his heart. She wasn't his real mother. She was his stepmother. She and her daughter Shayla had come into his father's life after his biological mother had died. Now she ruled the roost here at Shangri-La, and that was just wrong.

He and Shayla had always been at daggers drawn. But Shayla was older and his brother Ricky had been forced to deal with her. Marc had flown under the radar, staying out of Shayla's way and pretending she didn't exist.

Poor Ricky had been battered daily by the attacks Shayla dealt out. Now that he looked back, he wondered how his brother had put up with it. If only he'd been there for Ricky more often. If only he'd taken some of the blows himself, maybe Ricky would still be alive.

Maybe. Sure. It was no use thinking 'maybe'.

So he'd come back to his ancestral home to find his stepmother and his stepsister about to throw away the Huntington legacy that was over a century old. No one could pay enough to make the sale worth it. At least, that was the way it seemed to him. They wanted to sell the place and go live it up in the Bahamas. As if money could make up for losing their heritage.

This was a no-go as far as he was concerned. It was not going to happen. This property belonged to generations of Huntingtons and these interlopers were not going to be allowed to ruin that. He was the only real Huntington here, and he was going to have to put a stop to it.

CHAPTER THREE

A FEW minutes later, dinner over, Torie had to brush past Marc in order to leave the room.

"Waiting to high-grade the leftovers?" she asked mockingly in a soft voice for only him to hear.

"That would lead to starvation with this greedy crew," he murmured back to her.

She'd meant to get past him and move on, but something in his smoky blue eyes caught at her and she paused, held in his gaze for a beat too long.

"I get first pick at all times," he added arrogantly. "Or I don't play at all."

She flushed. He was so obviously trying to rattle her, and, darn it all—it was working. She should have known it was very foolish to taunt the tiger. A sharp retort came to mind, but she bit her lip and held it back, flipping her hair over her shoulder with a toss of her head and looking away as she walked on.

She could feel his gaze follow her like a brand on her back, but she just kept going. She'd come here to Shangri-La with a purpose—she wanted to find facts and clear her father, and that meant snooping into things. It might be best not to tempt Marc with reasons for him to want to follow her around.

She needed to stay as far away from this man as she could manage.

She joined the others on the wide terrace. The rain had cleared out the fog and now it had gone away as well. Twilight wasn't far off, and in the light that remained, Marge suggested they all join her in an excursion to the pier. She wanted to show them the boathouse and the dock. They all gathered into a group and began the long tramp down to the shore, but Torie noticed that Carl had slipped away and she hung back.

"I want to run up and get a jacket," she told Marge. "I'll catch up with you."

Just before she started up the stairs, she heard a muffled thumping down the hallway, and she followed the sound into the library. There was Carl, knocking on wooden panels as though he expected one to slide open at his touch.

"Searching for a secret compartment?" she asked a bit caustically. "Not cool, Carl."

He whirled to face her, his thin face intense. "Just checking the quality of construction," he said unconvincingly.

"I'll tell you what the construction is like," she responded, a bit impatient with him. "It's old. This place was built about a hundred years ago. And it's held up all this time. I wouldn't worry about how sound it is. If you buy it, obviously, you'll have to get some expert advice. Structural engineers and architects."

"Yes, of course," he said, frowning at her as though she were being a nuisance. He hesitated, then sighed and moved closer so that he could whisper. His dark eyes were darting about the room, strangely impatient. "But these old houses have false fronts and hidden passageways. I'm just checking it out." He frowned at her. "Did you know about any? Did you ever find one?"

She shook her head. He was really turning out to be a little strange, wasn't he?

"Carl, I never even came into this house when I lived on the property. My father worked here, but I didn't. We lived down by the gate, at the butler's house. I never even came onto the porch."

"You're sure?"

"I'm sure."

He gestured toward a glass cabinet in the corner of the room.

"So you never saw the bag of Spanish gold they used to keep in that display case?"

She turned and stared at it. An empty showcase was a sad thing and she realized it must have looked that way for the last fifteen years. Why had they left it like this? Did they think the Don Carlos Treasure would turn up again someday? From what she understood, it was at the bottom of the sea.

"No," she said softly. "I never saw it." At least not there.

There was a noise in the hallway and suddenly Jimmy, the current butler, appeared in the doorway, looking surprised to see them in the library. Torie gave him a friendly smile and told Carl, "I'm just running up to get a jacket. You ought to go on out and meet the others. They're taking a look at the old boathouse. You might just be interested."

Carl nodded, but he was eyeing Jimmy speculatively, and Torie took the opportunity to escape before he began questioning the man about construction facts. She raced up the stairs to the bedroom and was about to reach for her velour hoodie when she noticed that Marc's denim jacket was still lying where she'd tossed it on the chair. She hesitated. Something about it appealed to her on a primitive level. She ought to get it back to him.

Instead, she found herself pulling it on and posing in front of the full-length mirror. It was big and heavy and rough and it looked completely wrong for her slender frame—and she knew she had better get it off before Carl came up and saw her in it. But she hugged it to herself, thinking it had a male smell that could be seductive if she let it be. For just a moment, she remembered how it had felt to be in Marc's arms, coming through the fog. That made her smile at herself in the mirror.

"Go ahead and wear it if you want to," Marc's deep voice said.

She whirled, gasping in shock. There he was, standing in the doorway to her bathroom, a pipe wrench in his hand. Her face went instantly to crimson and she shed the jacket as though it had just caught on fire.

"What are you doing here?" she cried out.

Surprised, embarrassed, humiliated—she was all three at once.

She could tell he was trying not to smile, but he just couldn't help himself, and when his grin broke out, it was wide and sardonic.

"Just a little sink repair," he said, waving the wrench at her. "I thought you'd gone down to the beach with the others."

She dropped the jacket on the floor and glared at him. "I hate you," she said unconvincingly.

He laughed, which only made her more angry. "Totally understandable," he acknowledged.

"I was just…just…" There was no way to explain what she'd been doing, prancing around in his jacket in front of her mirror, so she gave it up. "You ought to let people know when you're in their bathroom."

He shrugged. "Exactly why I came out when I did. I wanted to make sure you didn't do anything you'd regret." He couldn't help but grin again. "I've got to admit, you look a hell of a lot cuter than I do in that jacket. Maybe you should keep it."

She glared at him. "I don't want it," she said emphatically as she threw it toward him. Her face was beginning to cool down. For a moment there she'd been afraid she would explode with the agony of it all. Things were better now—heart rate slowing, skin cooling, breathing getting back to normal. Maybe she was going to be okay.

"What were you really doing in here?" she asked him, frowning suspiciously. "Checking around for some answers to those questions you were talking about?"

"Why?" He cocked a curious eyebrow her way. "Are there some answers lurking where I could find them?"

Her green eyes narrowed. "You tell me."

He shook his head as though she thoroughly amused him. "I didn't go through your things," he told her patiently. "And I really don't plan to. Not yet anyway."

She glared at him. "Not ever!"

He considered her words for a moment. "How about this?" he said. "You go ahead and give me some answers now. Then I won't be tempted to go digging at all."

She hesitated, searching his smoky eyes for reasons to believe he was being straight with her. What would he be digging for, anyway? Did he really think she was some kind of scam artist? Or that Carl was?

That gave her pause. After all, she wasn't too sure about Carl herself anymore.

"We could try that," she said, attempting to sound reasonable and watching his reaction. "We could both ask each other. Take turns."

He made a face as though he thought that was going a little far, but still he said, "If you want."

"Ask me something," she challenged. "I'll see if you deserve an answer or not."

He nodded, considering. "And I'll see if I can trust anything you tell me."

Her chin rose and her eyes blazed. "Trust is a slippery thing."

"You got that right." He carefully put the wrench down on the desk. "Okay, let's just try it." He shrugged. "You start."

She thought for a second, then said, "Here's one. Why are you so mean?"

He threw his head back and groaned. "That's such a girlie question. There's no way I can answer that."

She shrugged, nose in the air. "I rest my case. You can't be trusted."

He glared at her. "You've got to ask things that get to substance, not feelings."

She glared back. "Okay, let's hear your great question."

"Okay." He looked at her for a long moment, then shoved his hands down into the pockets of his jeans and frowned. "Here's what I want to know. Why would you lie about being married?"

Her heart flipped over and began to pound. Her hands curled into fists. "So now you're calling me a liar?" she said breathlessly.

"Oh yeah. Beyond a doubt."

She flushed. What could she say? He was right. "You're just grasping for things to make me angry," she charged, knowing it was a weak one. "You don't have any proof."

"I don't need proof. I've got common sense and my own two eyes." He gave her a half smile. "In fact, I've got a whole list of reasons that tell me you two aren't married."

"A list?"

"Yeah."

She turned away, panic fluttering in her throat. "You know, I don't need this…" she began, but a shout from the direction of the beach stopped the words in her throat and they both went out onto the balcony, looking toward where the sound had come from.

"They've started back," Marc said. "Looks like you missed your tour of the boat house."

They both leaned on the railing, looking

west and watching a gorgeous sunset. All traces of the fog were gone now, and the sky was streaked with red and purple. The ocean was silver blue.

Marc rubbed his eyes as though they were tired and he looked again, shaking his head. "It's so damn beautiful," he said softly, almost to himself. "I'd forgotten how much I loved the evening sky out here."

She looked at him sideways. "You haven't been back here much lately?"

"No. Not at all, in fact. I've mostly been overseas."

She thought about that for a minute. If she'd come earlier, he wouldn't have been here. And that would have been a good thing. Wouldn't it?

"When did you get discharged from the military?"

"A while back. But I only came home two days ago." His mouth twisted. "I've been gone over ten years and it all still looks so much the same. You'd think the land would show the scars of…" He winced, then shrugged, letting the thought go. "Anyway, I can't believe how much this place means to me. I can see my history everywhere I look."

He pointed. "See that broken gate to the

rose garden? See how it lists? That happened when I told my high-school sweetheart I wasn't the marrying kind. She slapped me and then slammed that poor gate so hard, it almost fell off the hinges."

Torie tried to remember who that would have been but the memory didn't surface. "At least you recovered," she murmured.

"Yeah. Sort of."

This time his grin was open and sweet and her heartbeat quickened just seeing it.

But he wasn't finished. "See that pile of rocks by the oak tree? That's where my brother and I buried our old dog Neville."

"Oh." Torie gasped. She'd forgotten about Ricky. Two years older than Marc, he'd been a shyer, more remote figure, sort of awkward and a bit of a computer geek. What had ever happened to Ricky?

"We had a funeral service and put that dear old dog in the ground," Marc said. He shook his head, a half smile lingering on his lips.

"Where is your brother?" she asked, hoping he would tell more.

He didn't answer for a long moment, and when he spoke again, his voice was gravelly. "Gone. I can't believe how long it's been. He died just over ten years ago."

"Oh no!"

The news went through her like an electric shock. It was horrible to think of Ricky gone. And all this time, she'd never known about it. She felt a trembling deep down that shook her. Ricky had never been anything much to her. Not the way Marc had been. She'd demonized him in her mind because he was part of her enemy—the Huntingtons. But was that fair? He was part of her past, too.

There was too much tragedy in the world. Ricky, Marc's father, her own father—all gone. Tears shimmered in her eyes and she covered her mouth with her hands, as though holding back the dark side of life for all she was worth.

He watched her for a moment, wondering why his brother's death would seem to touch her like this. That was a part of the fascination he had with her—she was always surprising him. Just when he thought he had her all figured out, she would do or say something that showed him how useless it was to make assumptions.

Turning, he looked out at the grounds again, searching for something he could use to change the subject.

"The red tile roof you see in the distance

used to be the butler's house," he pointed out, hoping to distract her.

It seemed to be working. She'd turned her attention to where he'd indicated.

"He had a little girl who used to hide in the apple tree while I was washing my car over there by the shed. She'd wait up there, eating apples, until the car was sparkling clean and I was gone and then she would throw the apple cores down on my just-washed car."

"No she did not!" Torie said before she thought. But it wasn't true! She would never have done such a thing. Would she?

He looked at her in surprise. "How would you know?"

She was flushing again and still wiping tears from her eyes. This was not a road she wanted him to go down. She had to change the subject and nip this in the bud.

Turning away, she went back into the room and sank down to sit on the bed. "Listen, you were going to tell me why you got this nutty idea that Carl and I weren't married," she reminded him. Better that than memories of the chubby little girl in the apple tree. "You said you had a list."

"That's right." He followed her back in,

standing in front of her and looking down at her. "You want to hear it?"

She took a deep breath and made herself smile. "Sure. And I'll shoot down every one of your items. Go."

"Okay." He cleared his throat. "To begin with, I'd say Carl has a passion, but it's not for you."

He said the oddest things!

"Gee thanks," she retorted.

He gave her a curious look. "I hope that doesn't break your heart."

"Hardly. Go on. I thought you had a whole list."

"I do. Here goes." His head tilted back and he began to go through the reasons, counting them off on his fingers.

"No ring on your finger. No ring on his. Separate bedrooms. You two sit at a dinner table like strangers. Newlyweds usually can't keep their hands off each other."

Her lower lip stuck out and she took a deep breath. "Circumstantial evidence. What else?"

He turned and held her gaze with his own for a long, long moment before he spoke. And then he said, in a soft, husky voice, "The way you look at me."

She gasped sharply and her cheeks colored again. "You don't play fair, do you?" she said breathlessly, looking at him wide-eyed, knowing she probably looked hurt rather than angry. Because that was pretty much the way she felt.

He hesitated. She could see the indecision in his eyes. Then he reached out and touched her cheek softly with his fingertips. One casual caress and his hand was gone again.

"Torie, I don't mean anything personal by that. I just mean that like any healthy young woman, you're attracted to men. Not just me. It could be anybody. You're not committed to one guy yet and it's written all over you."

He was so right about everything—probably why he was annoying. The more he talked, the less she found she could argue back about.

Still, this was not fair. She turned back to glare at him. "It's all none of your business, you know."

"Wrong." He shrugged, his eyes cool and mysterious. "You came here under false pretenses. You claimed something that isn't true. I should send you packing."

She drew in a quick breath. "No. Your mother can do that if she wants. But you have no standing to do it. You didn't invite us."

"I didn't invite you," he repeated, shaking his head. The bitter twist was back in his mouth. "You're right. It's up to my mother. If she doesn't care that you lied to get in here, why should I?"

Her courage took on new life. "You got that right. Good for you."

"Tell me this, Torie." He moved closer, looking down into her eyes. "Just exactly why are *you* here?"

"Me?"

"Yes. You." He shook his head. "You're not married to Carl. You don't care if he buys the place or not. What do you want out of all this?"

"I…" She closed her eyes and swayed a bit. She wanted to tell him the truth. She wanted to tell him that she'd lived here in the past, that if he thought hard, he would remember her, that his family had ruined her family and they ought to face that fact—and help her get to the truth. That was what she wanted. But she didn't have the proof to back up those claims. Not yet. Soon, she hoped to lay it all before him. Very soon.

"I'm helping Carl," she said. "Believe it or not, he thinks he needs me. He thinks portraying himself as a married man gives him more gravitas to make his case and submit his purchase plans."

"No." He shook his head slowly, his gaze travelling over her face as though sure the truth was in there somewhere. "That's not it. I don't think Carl wants to buy Shangri-La at all. He doesn't have that land-grab look in his eyes."

She threw out her hands, palms up. "Okay Mr. Know-It-All, then what *did* we come here for?" She waited, breathing fast. What was he going to guess? Did he have any idea?

"You got me." His blue eyes searched her dark ones. "I don't know. I don't know why you came. I don't know what you were doing out at the caves. I don't know who you really are. But I intend to find out." He flashed her a lopsided grin, his eyes filled with mischief. "So be careful, baby. Just remember. Like the song says, every move you make."

"You'll be watching me," she said, trying to keep the resentment out of her voice but not entirely succeeding. "Got it."

CHAPTER FOUR

"WHAT was that?" Lyla's coal-black eyes were wide and startled. Her stylishly short hair was swept back in two wings at the sides of her face, making her look all the more surprised. "Was that a wolf?"

It was well after dark and Jimmy had started a fire in the fire pit on the patio overlooking the ocean. The others were gathering there, and Torie had joined them. The strange, high-pitched cry, wild and unnerving, had come during a lull in conversation.

"It sounds like a coyote," she told the pretty woman reassuringly. "They usually shy away from humans. I wouldn't worry about it."

"Hey, no problem," the man named Frank told her with a leering smile. "No one's going to let a lovely lady like you get eaten by wolves."

"Define *wolves*," his wife Phoebe interjected caustically, looking daggers at Lyla.

Torie turned away. She was definitely staying out of this one. The drinks had been flow-
ing freely for over an hour now, so the voices
were getting higher and laughter was ringing
throughout the patio area. That was good as
far as she was concerned. At some point, she
was hoping to feel safe in slipping away and
following her own plan. It was just a matter
of time.

She sank down into a deep wicker chair,
staring into the golden flames that were leap-
ing higher and higher, ignoring the others and
letting memories creep up out of her subcon-
scious.

She remembered parties around this very
fire pit—but not parties that she ever attended.
She remembered slinking about in the shadows, watching as Ricky or Marc gathered here
with their high-school friends, envying them
their abandoned joy, wishing…she wasn't sure
what. But wishing with all her heart anyway
for something…someone.

She glanced out into the trees, wondering
if there was anyone watching the way she'd
watched. Sure enough, there was Marc. He
wasn't exactly hiding the way she had, but he
was watching. Right now, he had his attention trained on someone else, though, and that

made her smile. He was so busy keeping tabs on everyone. What made a man so paranoid?

But she knew very well what did that. It affected her, too.

He glanced her way and her gaze met his and she made a face, hoping to annoy him. Then she winked, for no reason at all. She caught the ghost of a smile on his face before he turned away and started watching the big Texan who was enthralling one and all with tales of his cowboy days herding cattle out on the range, heading for the Chicago stockyards.

"Has this guy ever heard that trains took over that job about a hundred years ago?" Frank muttered as he walked past her.

She glanced around the circle. Once again, Carl had disappeared and she frowned. What was his problem, anyway?

Someone put a stick in her hand and she noticed, vaguely, there was something white attached to the end of it.

"Oh my gosh," Lyla cried out as someone handed her one too. "Toasted marshmallows on a stick. Are you serious?"

Torie blinked, realizing she was right. Dutifully, she began waving it toward the flames but she wasn't particularly interested in the results.

"You're letting it burn," a low voice said from behind. Marc had come in from the cold and he reached out and took the stick from her, turning it expertly so that it browned evenly. He handed it back.

She gave him a questioning look, then stared at the gooey mess on the end of her stick. "I'm supposed to eat this?"

"You'll love it."

"I doubt it."

He took it off the stick and popped it into her mouth before she could stop him. That made her laugh. It was good, sugary and crisp on the outside, creamy on the inside, and delicious in a simple, childish way.

"Okay, now you have to eat one," she said.

The look on his face told her it would be a cold day before that happened.

"Where's Carl?" he asked, looking around at the others.

That reminded her. He thought she was a crook, and if he knew who her father was, that would probably clinch the deal in his mind. She had to be careful.

"You got me," she responded to his question about Carl. "There's no telling where he's gone or what he's up to."

He gave her a quizzical look, then shook

his head, looking at her so intensely, she felt suddenly chilled.

"Let's get out of here," he said, his voice low.

Something surged in her chest. "What? You and me?"

"Yeah." His eyes shone in the shadows. "I want to talk to you. Alone."

She felt the pull he had over her, but she could resist that. She bit her lower lip, thinking fast. She didn't have time to talk. She had to get going on her plan, and she didn't want him following her.

The first thing she wanted to do was to get to the house she'd lived in as a child, the one with the red tile roof, and do a little exploring. Luckily, Jimmy wasn't living in it and it seemed to be empty. In fact, it seemed no one had lived in it for years. All the better for finding something left behind that might ignite a memory or her imagination in ways that could help her.

"I don't think that will work," she said, looking away. "People will notice."

"And you care? Why?"

She frowned at him. "Because I'm a decent person, Marc. I want people to notice *that*. Maybe you don't. But I do."

Funny what amazing thoughts came tumbling out of her head because she felt she had to fight back against him. She'd never thought this position over, but now it seemed to be hers.

"And there's something else," she told him. "Look into my eyes. Do you see someone who's attracted to you?" She glared at him. "Do you see someone who looks susceptible to your load of bull? Because I don't. And I want you to acknowledge it."

He stared at her and shook his head as though he thought she was nuts. "Okay," he said. "Point taken. I was wrong. You don't have a thing for me. I can accept that."

"Can you, Marc?" She glared harder. "Good. Because I don't have a crush on you. So don't expect it."

His mouth twisted in half a grin. "All right. Sorry I ever brought it up."

"Okay." She took a deep breath.

His mouth twisted and his gaze was sardonic. "But you're still not married to Carl. Isn't that right?"

She sighed and tossed her head, letting her hair fly behind her, then looked toward the fire. When she looked back, he was gone.

* * *

But he wasn't far away. Every nerve ending he possessed, every element of caution, was on edge. There was something going on here. He could feel it in the air. He wasn't sure what it was—but he was going to find out.

Was Torie involved? Undoubtedly. His gaze kept getting pulled back to her, leaving him halfway between bemused and annoyed. Something about her nagged at him—as though there was something he'd forgotten, something he'd filed away and put into the wrong drawer. Something just didn't compute. Why did she look so familiar?

And where the hell was Carl? A part of him wanted to go looking for him, but then Torie would disappear. Better to stay. Someone had to keep an eye on her.

She spoke to the Texan and laughed at something he said back, but her gaze quickly returned to search him out. What expression did he see on her face? Defiance? Anger? He wasn't sure what it was, but it only aroused his interest. He couldn't stop looking at her. She was getting ready to make a move and he wanted to be sure he knew about it when it happened.

But the night was young and Marge had plans for them all.

"Come on, everybody," she announced, calling them all to gather around the fire pit. "I've got Jimmy bringing in more wood. We'll sit around the fire and tell stories."

"Ghost stories?" Lyla asked, looking worried.

"No," Marge said, laughing. "Let's get back to the reason you're all here. I think each of you should talk about Shangri-La and what you would do to change it into your own special dream. How about that?"

Torie couldn't hide her smile. Marge was turning out to be quite a saleswoman. She glanced over at where Marc was standing, a beer in his hand, looking watchful.

Of course, she thought. *I'm surely not the only one he's got his eye on tonight, and that's obvious.*

Marge was trying to perk the party up, to generate some enthusiasm among the people crowding close to the fire, trying to get warm.

"Come on people. Dig deep. Think back. Recall patio parties and fireplace sing-alongs from your early days. Think of the potential here." She looked at the faces turned her way. "Come on, Lyla," she said. "What would you do if you owned this place?"

Lyla smiled, looking dreamy, and stepped

out into the light. "I see this property as a setting for an entertainment center. I'd set up a stage and put on theatrical performances, drawing audiences down from the Bay Area and up from Los Angeles."

"Lots of luck on that one," the Texan chortled. "Both of those are long drives. You'll get an audience of ten or so per show."

Lyla shrugged elaborately. "I'll start with that. But we would grow. Word of mouth…"

"Here's my plan," Phoebe chimed in happily. "I would love to have a spiritual retreat for our friends. Some are show-business people, some are politicians. They could come here and be refreshed by nature. I would put in a natural swimming pool right here, with a waterfall and vines hanging over it. I would have Greek statues all around the water."

"That sounds like Hearst Castle."

"Yes. I love Hearst Castle."

"That's okay if you're as rich as Hearst was," the Texan said. "Otherwise, better aim a little lower, I'd say. Stop dreaming."

"A human must dream," Andros protested grandly. "We have a dream too, me and Nina. We would make this place into a first-class destination resort for Mediterranean clients, people who want something different.

Our restaurant would be the core project, of course. We would make the best Greek restaurant in the world, right here, an old-fashioned supper club. And we would turn the house into a hotel…."

Nina chimed in, telling them about her ancient recipes handed down through the family grandmothers. "Old-country charm supported by modern technology," she declared. "We have such plans."

"No way," the Texan said dismissively. "You're all aiming to go broke in the first year."

"Oh yeah?" Frank retorted. "Then what's your idea, cowboy? A dude ranch?"

"Hell no. I have no interest in drawing other people here. The first thing I'll do is hire a geologist and a mining engineer and start drilling holes."

"Holes?"

That got everyone's attention and they all stared at him raptly.

"Sure. We would tear this place apart. I'm bettin' on gold, lady. There was a pretty good vein that tapped out in the nineteenth century not far from here. I'm bettin' we can track it down and…"

"Are you serious?" Marc said, frowning fiercely.

"California gold. That's what the state is known for. There's gotta be some somewhere. I'm bettin' on these here hills."

"You're crazy," Frank said, and four or five other voices joined in, each with a different view of the possibilities of finding gold.

"How about you, Torie?" Marge asked as the argument died down. "What do you and Carl have in mind?"

Torie tried to deflect the question. She didn't want to get caught up in this. "You'll have to ask Carl himself for that."

All eyes were turned her way.

"We're asking you," Frank pointed out.

"Me?"

"Sure. Aren't you involved?"

"Oh. Sure." She cleared her throat. What the heck could she say? She had no idea what Carl would want. Everyone was waiting. She felt cornered.

But then it came to her—not Carl's dream, but her own. It was a picture of what Shangri-La had been twenty years before when she'd been a child. She realized now how much she'd loved it, how central it had been to her universe—the core of her being—the place that had molded her identity.

"If I had this place all to myself," she began, staring off at the moon drifting off over the ocean and leaving a trail of silver behind, "I would build a trellis along the walkway at the top of the cliff and grow wild roses all through it."

She went on, caught up in the memories, and conjured up every detail of what the place had looked like in its glory days, when she was a child. Just bringing back those pictures made her heart sing. She smiled as she talked and wondered if this was what love felt like.

Marc grimaced as Torie began, tempted to go look for Carl while he knew she was occupied. He had to stop falling for the spell she seemed to weave so easily in his head and in his body. But he hesitated, and once she'd started talking, he was really listening to her words. Frowning, he concentrated. What she was saying sliced through him like a knife. The picture she was painting was one he recognized. It fit his childhood.

She knew this place. She'd been here before.

He looked over to see if his stepmother had noticed, but her attention was wrapped up in smiling at Jimmy. That made his stomach turn and he swore softly, shaking his head. Then he looked back at Torie.

Who the hell was she anyway?

Torie came out of her reverie and looked around. Everyone was staring at her and she felt her cheeks heating up. What had she said that seemed to have enthralled them all?

Her gaze met Marc's. He looked as though he couldn't believe what he'd been hearing, and then he jerked his head in a way that told her he wanted to talk to her privately. Something in the look on his face made her think she might want to comply this time.

She waited until the conversation began to buzz around the fire again. And when no one seemed to be paying any attention to her, she rose and slipped out of the firelight, meeting Marc on the walkway through the palms.

"What is it?" she said as she came up to him.

He was standing with his arms crossed over his chest, staring at her. "Who are you?" he demanded.

She drew in her breath and her pulse began to sputter. "I'm…I'm just Torie…"

"Torie who? What's your real last name?"

She started to speak and he stopped her.

"Don't give me that Marino nonsense. Your *real* last name."

She shook her head, looking away. The masquerade hadn't lasted very long, had it? "Listen Marc…."

"No, you listen. That little tale you spun out there by the fire was a perfect description of what this place used to look like twenty years ago. How did you know that?"

She tried to smile but his eyes weren't friendly at all. She had a sinking feeling inside. She wasn't very good at this deception stuff. She couldn't possibly tell him everything, but maybe she could let a few things go.

"I used to live here," she told him frankly.

He stared at her, shaking his head.

"It's true. I'm Torie Sands."

"Sands? As in…?"

She drew in a deep breath and came clean. "Jarvis Sands was my father."

He stared at her. "The butler."

"Yes."

"The one who stole the Don Carlos Treasure."

"No!" she said fiercely. "He never did. He was falsely accused."

Marc's head went back. "As I remember it, he went to jail…."

"He was never formally indicted and the treasure was found. He was released." She shook her head, wishing her eyes weren't stinging with tears. How could her emotions about that time be so close to the surface when it was so long ago? "It was all a horrible mistake."

He was frowning, his gaze ranging over her face, studying every feature as though he could randomly rearrange them and get to the truth. "You used to live in the gatehouse."

She nodded, holding herself together with effort.

"Your name wasn't Torie though, was it?"

"No. It was Vicki." She shrugged. "Actually, Victoria."

He was looking at her in wonder. "You were the chubby little girl who used to throw things at me from the apple tree."

"I never threw anything at you," she replied, wishing she didn't sound as though she were pouting. "But I was that little girl."

"Vicki Sands." He nodded slowly. "Sure, I see it now. That *was* you." He shrugged as though hardly knowing what to think. "I can't believe it." His gaze sharpened. "So what are you doing here, Torie? Why did you come back?"

She searched his handsome face and considered telling him the truth. She wanted to. But was that smart? After all, what she was here for was to prove his family wrong. He wasn't going to help her do that, was he? The best thing that could come out of this was if she could convince him to leave her alone and let her get on with it. She wasn't going to get anywhere with him hanging around.

She shrugged and looked away. "Nostalgia, I guess. I thought it would be fun to see the old place again."

"Really." His skeptical take on her statement was obvious. "I see." His head tilted to the side as he considered her words. "So that's why you went straight for the caves. It had something to do with the Don Carlos Treasure. Of course."

"No." She turned, wanting to defend her actions, but she saw the disbelief in his eyes and she was glad she'd kept the truth to herself. "Actually, I went out there because I used to play in those caves and I wanted to see them again. For old time's sake."

"Right."

He didn't believe her but she tried to get

past that. After all, what did she care if he didn't believe her? All she really wanted from him was to be left alone. Still, there was something she had to say.

"I…I heard about what happened to your father," she told him. "And despite everything, I was sorry he had to go that way."

He frowned. "What do you mean, despite everything?"

She blinked at him. Didn't he remember how it was? His father had been the one who'd had hers arrested. There was certainly cause for her to resent the man. Her father had loved working for Hunt, as they called him, and had felt personally close to him. The way his old friend had turned on him had seemed a complete betrayal. It was a major factor in his taking his own life.

She frowned and turned away, fighting back emotion, but he didn't seem to notice that she hadn't answered.

"Wait. I'm trying to remember. Didn't your father die shortly after you moved back down to Los Angeles that year?" he asked her. "I thought my father had told me that."

She nodded, holding tears back with all the strength she had. There was no way she was going to cry in front of him.

"Yes," she said gruffly. "My mother always says he died of a broken heart." She coughed, covering up how her voice was shaking. "But actually…actually…" She turned and looked right into his face. "Actually, he shot himself."

"Oh God." His face registered pure compassion for a moment, and he reached out and touched her arm. "I'm sorry, Torie. I don't think I knew that."

She shrugged, forcing back the lump in her throat and pulling away from his hand.

"Funny," he said softly. "So both our fathers committed suicide. How strange."

"Oh!" She stared at him. His eyes looked troubled in the dark. "I didn't know. The papers didn't say… I thought…"

"It was an accidental drowning? Yeah, we got that announced and it stuck, luckily. But he left a note. We knew he died on purpose."

She felt as though she'd been slugged in the stomach. She'd had no idea. She'd spent a lot of time resenting the man, but to hear he'd been tortured enough to want to end it all changed a lot in her heart.

Impulsively, she reached out and took his hand. "Oh Marc, I'm so sorry. I didn't know."

He gazed down into her face. Tears still shimmered in her eyes. He looked at her pretty mouth and everything in him hungered to kiss her. Why? Just because she was pretty? Just because she was so close? No matter how much she appealed to him, she wasn't available. She might not be married to Carl, but that didn't mean she was free.

Deliberately, he pulled away from her touch.

"Carl," he said, reminding himself as well as her. "What's the deal with him? What's he looking for?"

She shook her head. "I really don't know. He hasn't told me." She hesitated, thinking fast. She needed to keep her cards close to her vest. She shouldn't tell him too much. "I thought he was interested in buying the place and wanted to check out all the details. And that's probably all it is."

"But you don't know."

She bit her lip. What could she say? "When you come right down to it, I don't really know him all that well," she admitted. There was no use trying to maintain the fiction that they had ever been married. It was too late for that.

"I've worked for him a few times. He found out I grew up here, so when he decided to come check it out, he asked if I wanted to come and pretend to be his wife."

She looked up into his eyes, hoping she was

coming across as undeniably innocent—because that was what she was. Wasn't she? Sure she was. She was using Carl, but he was using her. They both knew the score. It was basically an arrangement of convenience for both of them.

"I thought it would be fun, so I agreed to come with him." She shrugged. "Other than that…"

A call came from the fire-pit area. It sounded as though the others were preparing to go to their rooms for the night. Torie's heart fell. She wouldn't have time to go to the old house and do the investigating she'd planned to do. Even if she could lose Marc, it was just too late. The others would be looking for her.

She gazed up at his face, surprised at how he seemed to get better-looking by the hour. Was it really him? Or was it her?

"I'd better get back," she said.

He nodded, but as she began to turn away, he caught hold of her arm and pulled her around to face him.

"Promise me one thing," he said huskily, his gaze hooded. "Keep your door locked tonight."

Her eyes widened. "You mean…?"

His grip on her arm tightened. "I mean keep your door locked. I don't trust Carl."

"Oh no. He would never…"

Something flickered in his eyes. "He's a man, isn't he? And you're a very attractive woman. I don't trust him. Lock that door."

She took a deep breath. For some reason, her heart was beating wildly. She didn't think of herself that way, and she didn't really believe he meant what he said about her. But still…

"Okay."

"I'm going to check it. I'll give you a knock like this…" He demonstrated against a handy tree trunk. "So you'll know it's me. Just checking."

She searched his eyes and shook her head. "Why are you doing this?"

He thought for a minute, his brow furrowed, and then he shook his head too. "You got me," he said. "I guess it's for old time's sake. After all, you're sort of like a baby sister to me. Aren't you?"

She laughed shortly. "No," she said emphatically.

He shrugged and his hand loosened on her arm. "Okay. I guess I just want to make sure you're okay."

She nodded. "Fine. I can accept that."

"Good."

He looked down and for one, heart-stopping moment, she was sure he was about to kiss her. Marc Huntington was going to kiss her. How many times had she dreamed of this moment? She waited, ready, lips slightly parted, heart beating like a jungle drum. He stared down at her for a long moment, and then something changed in his eyes and he turned away.

"Good night, Victoria Sands," he said gruffly. "Sleep well. I'll see you in the morning."

And he melted into the shadows of the trees.

Her breath was coming fast, as though she'd just been running hard, and her face was burning. She felt like a fool. When would she ever learn? Marc Huntington was not for her. Never would be.

Back at the house, she managed to evade Carl as she passed the fire pit and made it all the way to her bedroom before he caught up with her.

"Hold it," he said, thrusting his shoulder in the way of her closing the door. "We've gotta talk."

"Carl, it's been a long day. I need to get some sleep."

"You can sleep all you want, but I need some help first. I need you to update the map."

She sighed. The map she'd drawn of the Shangri-La estate was rough at best. She'd done it from memory and given it to him back when they were first planning this little adventure. In some ways it had been a labor of love and she'd enjoyed dredging up all her old stories as she worked on it.

"What's missing?" she asked.

"The caves." He pulled a folded paper out of his jacket and looked at her quizzically, his gaze cold. "I'm just wondering. Why did you leave out the caves?"

That was a good question and she wasn't really sure what the answer was.

"Listen Carl, just leave the map with me and I'll get them sketched in by lunch tomorrow."

"No," he said, a hint of anger beginning to surface in his voice. "I need it tonight. I need…"

"Is there a problem?"

They both jumped and turned to find Marc coming down the hall toward them.

"Something I can do to help?" he asked silkily, staring at Carl.

Carl grabbed his map back and shoved it into his jacket, shaking his head and looking resentful. "No. It's nothing." He began to retreat toward his own room. "Okay, Torie. We'll deal with it in the morning. See you then."

She looked at Marc and he raised an eyebrow. "I know," she told him. He didn't have to say it. "Lock my door. Don't worry. I will."

And he was right, she mused as she prepared for bed. Carl had seemed so harmless when she'd agreed to come on this trip, but he'd changed. There was an intensity in Carl she'd never noticed before. She wasn't sure if she could say that she trusted him any longer.

She knew Marc didn't. But then, he didn't trust her either, did he?

Later, as she drifted into sleep, she thought she heard shouting. She sat up and tried to analyze what it was, but the sounds had faded by the time she was awake enough. Maybe she'd dreamed it. She lay back down but what little sleep she got after that was fitful. It was hard to let go when she knew that she was planning to get up and go exploring in a couple of hours anyway.

* * *

Plans that looked easy to execute from a distance always looked so impossible once you got face to face with the time to act. It was 1:00 a.m. and Torie's eyes were wide open, waiting for her little buzzer alarm on her cell phone to sound.

She felt as if she hadn't slept a wink. A part of her tried to justify just rolling over and going back to sleep, but she'd come all this way and she knew she couldn't miss this chance.

Her heart was beating in her throat. Was she really going to do this? Was she really going to start sneaking around, looking for information? Maybe it would be better to wait until morning when the light would be better and she could just be casual and find people to ask questions of.

"Coward!"

She said the word aloud, goading herself into action as the buzzer sounded and she reached out to stop it. She couldn't let this opportunity pass without taking advantage of it.

"Carpe diem," she added firmly, just for fun. Yes, she would seize the day. What else had she come for, anyway?

CHAPTER FIVE

TORIE slipped out of bed and reached for her clothes, pulling on leggings and a heavy sweatshirt that came down almost to her knees. She tied her hair back quickly and went to the doorway, opening it as quietly as she could. This was an old house. Just how badly were the stairs going to creak? She stayed as close to the banister as she could get and hardly made a sound.

The rooms downstairs were silent. She hesitated at the door, waiting for something to stop her, but nothing moved. Once out the door, she was free.

Now she was on a path she knew well. She didn't even have to think about it. Her feet knew where to step. She'd taken this route so many times in her childhood.

The night was clear and even though there was no moon visible, there was enough light to see where she was headed. The sounds of the frogs and crickets, the scent of the ocean, the breeze on her face—it all was so familiar, she found herself smiling as she hurried toward her old house as though she was truly going home. She rounded a corner and ducked back off the path as the flash of headlights from a passing car hit close to her. Who in the world was driving around at this time of night? From the snatch of laughter she heard, she could make a guess. Marge and Jimmy had been out and about.

She turned back and looked at her goal. Almost there. She stopped behind a small stand of palms to get the lay of the land, and she stood very still, shivering. Was it the cool air or a nervous reaction? For a moment, she thought about Marc and wondered what he was doing right now. Was he asleep? She certainly hoped so.

Finally she was on the front porch, the one she'd run onto as a girl, calling out, "Hey, Mom, what's for lunch?" as she threw down the latest shells she'd collected at the beach, or the prettiest rocks she'd found in the hills. The flame of nostalgia made her ache inside, but it was a good ache. Those were good days.

She tried the front door. It was locked. That was hardly surprising. Never mind. She knew other ways to get in. She made her way to the back of the house and found the window to her old room. It looked firmly closed and solid as a rock, but she knew that a little push here and a jiggle there and a shove in the right direction would loosen the sash and the window would slide up easily. She hadn't forgotten how to climb through, and in another minute, she was in her old room.

Pulling out her little flashlight, she played it against the empty walls. It was amazing, but no one had painted the rooms since her family had left. There was her growth chart by the door, milestones marked off in pencil. And there was the splotch of purple color where she'd thrown a paintbrush at the wall in a fit of anger. She stood and stared, breathless. Here it was, evidence that she really had lived here. For some reason, that choked her throat and filled her eyes with tears.

She went out into the hall and then the family room. The scrapings where chairs had brushed the walls, the mark on the door where her old dog Nanny had scratched to go out a few too many times, the old bulletin board where her mother had put up bits and pieces of her schoolwork or articles that interested her—all were still there. Had she stepped back in time?

The kitchen tore apart that theory. There was ample evidence that people had lived here since her day. The refrigerator was not the one she knew. The cabinets had been painted white and a relatively new-looking microwave sat on the counter.

That set her head back on straight. This wasn't her house. But she did have things she needed to do here.

The attic. That had been her goal from the beginning and she made her way through the living room to the hallway where the little structure that held the attic ladder hung from the ceiling. And how, without a stepladder or a piece of furniture, was she supposed to reach it to pull it down?

Her heart sank and she looked down the hallway and around the room. The heating register stood out against the wall, and there, leaning against it, was a long handled iron key for working the temperature controls. Could it possibly be long enough?

It was. She bit her lip as she worked hard to release the little rickety ladder, and her work paid off. It unfolded before her eyes, giving her access to the attic door. She climbed up quickly and tried to shove the door open. It didn't budge. She pushed and pulled and tried to pry it open, but nothing seemed to work.

And then she heard footsteps…a man's footsteps. She doused her little flashlight and pulled her legs up into the enclosure, heart racing. Anyone who came into the hallway would notice the ladder was down. But would they look up and see her perched there?

The footsteps came into the hallway. She tried to hold her breath, but she was already short of oxygen and rapidly falling into panic mode. Luckily, he just didn't stop walking, moving back and forth, just out of sight, making too much noise to hear her and her problems. The beam from his flashlight skittered around the walls, but didn't aim her way. She caught a glimpse of a shoulder in a black pea coat at one point, but she couldn't see enough to identify the man. All he had to do was glance up and she would be caught.

Suddenly, he stopped moving. Her heart nearly jumped out of her chest. Had he seen her?

No. He switched off his flashlight. He'd heard something, or had a sudden idea, because he turned and began to stride quickly toward the door. Now she was afraid he would get away before she could see who he was, and she slid down the ladder and sneaked silently toward the front room.

He was headed down the driveway toward the highway. She slipped out into the night and tried to stay hidden in the trees, following him the best she could. Was it Marc? Or Carl? She still couldn't tell.

So when the strong arms grabbed her from behind, she was completely unprepared and let out a shriek before the hand slapped down hard over her mouth.

"Hush," Marc growled in her ear. "It's me."

Her heart stopped and then started up again. She sighed, relaxing in his arms. It was just Marc. Everything was okay.

She tried to rouse her own sense of jeopardy. After all, what made her think Marc was a good guy? Still, his arms felt right around her and she turned her head to feel the heat of his face against her cool cheek as though she'd been waiting for just that.

"Torie, I'm not going to hurt you," he told her huskily, and she nodded.

"I know," she whispered back, even though she really had no reason to know that at all. She couldn't stop shivering and he held her more tightly against his body as though to calm her.

For just a moment, he indulged himself and turned his face into her hair. She smelled good and she felt even better. He didn't want to let go. He wanted to hold her and run his hands up under her sweatshirt and…

But he wasn't going to. Too tempting. Too stupid. Too dangerous. And most of all, a big distraction from what he had to do.

Instead, he slowly released her and she turned to face him.

"Hi," she said, peering at him in the dark. The features of his face looked as though they'd been cut from stone. "What are you doing here?"

"Looking for you, I guess," he said, his voice laced with sarcasm.

She frowned. "Who was that man?" she asked him. "I couldn't get a good look at him."

His mouth twisted. "Don't you know?"

"No! Was it Carl?"

"Weren't you meeting him out here?"

"Marc!" She threw up her hands in exasperation. "No, I wasn't meeting him. I wasn't meeting anyone. I'm actually surprised to find so many people out wandering around in the middle of the night." She glanced suspiciously into the trees. "I wonder who else is out there."

Marc glanced in the same direction. "There's no telling, but I wouldn't be too surprised to find a Texan, doing placer samplings here and there."

She smirked at him with impetuous impertinence. "Are you watching him, too?"

He surprised her with a sudden grin. "No. The man's an open book. I don't have to."

"Unlike me and Carl," she said, eyes flashing a sense of barely concealed resentment.

He didn't bother confirming her accusation, but it was more than true. He'd been following Carl when he'd come across Torie doing the same and he had to make the call—the lady or the tiger? He could only choose one. He'd gone with the one he would rather be with, and that had probably been a mistake.

See? Too tempting. Too dangerous.

Still, he might be able to get information out of her he would never get out of Carl. From what he could tell, there was little rhyme or reason for the way Carl was zigzagging all over the estate, looking for who-knew-what. What he couldn't figure out was—why was Torie tailing the guy as well?

"Just what is Carl looking for?" he asked her again.

She shrugged. "You got me."

He frowned. "You're the one who brought him here."

"No. I used him to get here, but that's as far as it goes."

He studied her as well as he could in the darkness. Basic instinct told him she was telling the truth. What the hell—he was going to take a chance on that instinct. It usually worked out best when he did, despite his natural inclination to want to see proof for everything.

"I wish I could figure the guy out," he told her. "I saw him leave the house and then I checked your room and you weren't there, so I took off after him."

"Where did he go?"

"Nowhere that made any sense."

She frowned. "So you thought you'd follow me for a while to see where I was going?"

"Why not?"

She groaned. "This is crazy. We're all running around in the middle of the night following each other. It's like a Keystone Kops episode. Going in circles, getting nowhere."

"I'm not getting nowhere." He gave her

a twisted smile and reached for her hand. "Come on."

"Where are we going?"

"Somewhere." His hand curled around hers as though he didn't trust that she would come along if he didn't force the issue. "Back into the house. I want to see what you were doing in there."

"No." She pulled back, obliging him to turn. "You know what? It's none of your business what I was doing in there. You can't stop me."

She knew she sounded childish. She felt childish. Maybe that all went along with her being in her childhood home. At any rate, it annoyed Marc enough that he yanked on her hand, pulling her in close and glaring down into her eyes.

"While you are here, you *are* my business. I thought we'd already established that. But in case you're still not convinced, let me say it again. I can kick you off the estate and send you home any time I want to. And I don't have to ask Marge first." He gave her that twisted smile again. "So be nice to me."

"I'm always nice," she protested, but her breath was coming faster.

"Prove it." His voice lowered huskily. "Tell

me why you're out here in the dark, dark night. Tell me what you hope to achieve."

She drew in a sharp breath. He was obviously stronger than she was and he could force her to go along with him if he wanted to. But he didn't need to force her. She could probably use his help. So she traded in complete rebellion for the chance to be a smart aleck instead.

"Wisdom," she said crisply. "Revenge. Closure. Truth."

He looked at her for a long moment and then he grimaced and his shoulders seemed to relax.

"That's a tall order," he said, his voice lighter. "Life doesn't usually give out free passes. I'm afraid you're probably going to have to work very hard for all those things, and never actually be satisfied with the results."

She closed her eyes, but a complete and detailed picture of him stayed in her mind. He had it all—looks, strength, a natural honesty that might be a façade, but was still impressive as hell. She wanted to trust him. Could she take that leap? She stared down at the hand that held hers and pondered that question.

Her first impulse was to keep it all to herself, not to let him in. But she didn't have time to wait this out. The only way she was going to get into the attic was if someone helped her. The only someone she could even half-way trust right now was Marc. Could she take the risk? What choice did she have? Besides, he was going to see the ladder and make his own assessment.

Should she go ahead and tell him? Why not? What did she have to gain by avoiding it? She made the decision and suddenly, she felt calm inside.

"Okay. Here goes." She raised her face to him again. "I'll tell you what I was doing. I was looking for something, anything, that might give me a new lead on finding out what really happened when my father was fired."

He stared down at her and shook his head. "Torie, that was a long time ago."

Her chin rose. "About time we got to the truth then."

He drew in a long, deep breath. "You really loved your father, didn't you?"

"Oh yes. Above all else."

He winced and she frowned, wondering why. Didn't he ever love anyone? Didn't he know how brave it could make you?

Or was it the other way around? Did he think no one had ever loved him that way?

She couldn't help all that. She had to move forward. If she could bring him along, so much the better.

The front door was standing open, just as she'd left it when she crept out. Moving quickly, they walked right in. Marc turned on his flashlight and did a quick survey of the empty room.

"There's nothing here. What's it been, fifteen years? What did you think you would find?" He looked at her. "Or were the walls going to talk to you? Spill all the secrets."

"I want to get into the attic," she told him. "The door seems to be sealed."

He moved closer, searching the depths of her green eyes. "What's in the attic?" he asked softly.

She had to steel herself not to start shivering again. "I'm not sure."

He shook his head. "You're going to have to do better than that. You must have something in mind."

She shrugged and it felt like surrender. She would tell him what she had to, but she couldn't tell him everything.

"My mother told me there were things left

in the attic," she said slowly. "I…we left in such a hurry, we couldn't take everything."

He nodded. "That was a long time ago," he noted again. "Other people have lived here since."

She took a deep breath and tried to smile. "I know. But I have to look and see." She met his gaze and tried to maintain her dignity, but she knew he could see the pleading in her eyes. "Please, Marc. I really need to see what's in the attic."

He gazed at her for a long moment. The sweet, quiet way she'd asked him made him want to help her more than anything else! If she would put away the threat of antagonism that always seemed just a comment away, they might get on quite well with each other.

He shrugged. "Let's go take a look."

To her chagrin, he shoved the attic door open with no problem at all and then followed her up into the dusty area. The light from his flashlight made eerie shadows as it flickered through the beams. The ceiling was low and they both had to bend over to make their way toward where boxes and old suitcases were stacked.

Torie sorted through the boxes quickly, then turned to the luggage. Most items belonged to other people, but there was a suitcase that looked familiar. Marc gave the locks a jab with his pocketknife and they sprang open.

Torie stared at what was inside, more moved than she'd expected. These were the remnants of another life, far, far away, but she recognized them immediately. Her mother's wool coat. Her own band uniform. Her father's sweaters.

And beneath all that, a photo album and a stack of papers. She went through the papers anxiously, heart beating. Marc watched her, wondering what she was looking for. He didn't ask again.

She'd set the photo album aside carelessly and he wondered why. He picked it up and leafed through it while she searched, holding the flashlight high. There was that chubby young girl Torie had once been. Seeing the pictures made him smile.

"How did you manage to make such a big change from the annoying little squirt you used to be?" he asked her dryly.

"Magic," she shot back, not looking up from her search. "I traded a cow for a handful of beans."

"Right."

The pictures showed a loving family living at Shangri-La—his home—and none of them were any relation to him. Sort of weird. Jarvis the butler was just as he remembered him—full dignity with a touch of reserve. He remembered Torie's mother, too, a pretty woman with a slightly worried, fragile look.

"Darn," Torie muttered at last, sitting back. "It's not here."

He waited for a moment, but she didn't say any more, and he moved impatiently.

"What? What are you looking for?"

She ignored him and began to put things back in the suitcase.

Assuming she would want the photo album, he held onto it.

"Take a look at these pictures," he said, opening the album to a shot of Torie in her younger, more rounded past.

She took a deep breath and shook her head, avoiding even looking his way. "I can't," she said, her voice strangely choked. "Not now. I just can't."

He watched her curiously, touched by the emotion he heard in her voice. Life hurt pretty much everybody, one way or another, but it seemed life had really done a number on Torie. Still, he couldn't believe she wouldn't want the pictures eventually. He tucked the album under his arm and led the way back down into the house.

"What now?" he asked her.

She looked tired and a bit defeated. Not finding whatever it was that she'd been looking for seemed to have crushed her for the time being. He had a fleeting thought that this might be the time to press her, to poke around in her psyche and get to the truth of what she was doing here, what she really hoped to accomplish. But when he looked at her sad, pretty face, he didn't have the heart for it. Maybe later.

"I guess I might as well go back to bed," she said, holding her chin high with seeming effort. "I can't really look any place else until it's light."

He raised an eyebrow. "Are you going to give me a hint?"

She glanced at him, then away. "What do you mean?"

"What are you looking for? What did you think you would find in that suitcase?"

She stared at him and he knew she was mulling over her options.

"You never know," he said softly. "I might have already found it. I might have hidden it myself."

"Hidden what?" she challenged, blinking rapidly.

He shrugged. "What you're searching for. Why don't you tell me what it is?"

She took a deep breath, looking at him sideways. He was sounding so reasonable and looking so gorgeous. It wasn't fair. Marc wasn't fair. He thought he could manipulate her. And maybe he wasn't far off the track. He had to know she'd always had a thing for him.

She had to convince him that all embers of that fire had gone cold long ago. And they had! After all, he was one of the people, one of the family, who had been so cruel to her father. She had to remember that.

But she was at a dead end. She'd searched the caves. She'd searched the attic. She had no other leads.

"My mother thinks my father had a journal," she said softly, avoiding his gaze. "She thinks he put things down that might help me—might show the way to the truth." She shook her head. "I don't know. I never saw it. I was just hoping…"

She stopped. Tears were choking her voice. He stared at her, wanting to take her in his arms. She looked so sad, so lonely. But he wasn't ready to give her the benefit of the doubt. Not yet.

What was it about this woman that seemed to crash right through all his normal defenses and touch him at his core? They were fighting over something here and he couldn't concede. Not without getting something for his side.

"I've never found a journal," he told her. At least he could be honest with her. "Are you sure it exists?"

She shook her head, avoiding meeting his gaze. "I'm not sure of anything." She looked up at him, tears shimmering in her haunted eyes. "I'm not even sure my father was innocent. What do you think of that?"

He raked his hard fingers through his hair, leaving spikes in every direction. He could see she was tortured and he wanted to grab her and hold her and tell her it was going to be okay—but he couldn't.

"I don't think," he told her, mostly because he didn't know what to think of that statement. "I just react."

She nodded. She shouldn't have said that. It was true, but no one else needed to know. She couldn't un-say it, but she could throw some other things out there into the mix to lessen its impact. Hopefully.

"Okay. React to this." She took a deep breath and her green eyes looked like bits of shattered emeralds. "I've hated your family for fifteen years. I think you caused my father's suicide. If it hadn't been for the way you all handled it and how disgraced you made him feel, he would be alive today." Her voice was firm, but the edges were trembling, just a little bit. "What's your side say?"

Her words stung. He turned away. His natural reaction was to lash out at her, but he held it back. She was talking crazy. Her words, her emotions, her reasoning, everything was jumping all over the place. She wasn't really making sense. And maybe that was because she really didn't have any solid proof of anything. It was all conjecture, all an attempt to fill in a past she just couldn't understand.

Understandable. Still, he had to balk when he heard her using his family as an excuse to cover up her family's heartbreak. But that didn't mean she wasn't in pain. He could see it. He could feel it. Her soul was writhing in agony.

And he had a sudden insight. If it was true what she'd told him, if she really didn't know for sure if her father was guilty, if this was more a search for truth than a search for proof—then she had a kind of inner integrity that was rare to find.

Still, it didn't mean she couldn't be capable of some pretty underhanded methods to get to where she wanted to go. He'd seen enough of the raw and untamed side of humanity to know it was always lurking. Never trust anyone. That was his motto.

"My father was an honorable man," he said softly, leashing his anger. "If he did something that hurt your father, I'm sure he had a reason. He didn't have a mean bone in his body."

Tears were sliding silently down her face. Her mouth twisted. "I know," she whispered. "I…I loved your father, too." Her voice broke. "He was so kind to me. I can't believe… Don't you see?" She hugged herself, arms wrapped tightly. "That's part of the problem. It just doesn't make sense that he would treat my father like an evil person. He…he…"

She couldn't go on. He started to reach for her, but she turned away. "Torie," he said, but she shook her head and moved further away.

"Let's go back." She started off down the trail. He followed close behind.

He wasn't sure what he wanted to do. Everything in him rebelled at her calling his father a villain. He didn't believe it. He'd known the man too well.

But at the same time, he suspected her father had probably been treated badly. Why? How? Had he really been guilty of the original theft? Or what? He wanted to get to the bottom of this as much as she did.

"By the way," he said as they walked along the path. "The Greeks have gone."

She stopped and whirled, staring up at him, remembering the shouts she'd thought she heard in the night.

"What? What happened?"

He shrugged. "Turns out they weren't very Greek. And they definitely weren't on the up and up."

Her shoulders sagged and her face was truly sad. "Oh no. I liked the Greeks."

"Sure you did," he said as they started off again. "That's part of their game. They spend a lot of time at events like this, or resort gatherings, endearing themselves to people with money and trying to get some of it."

She sighed sadly, looking up at the house as they approached. All the windows were dark. Hopefully everyone was asleep—even Marge and Jimmy. "So there's no idyllic little Greek supper club?"

"No."

"No little Greek grandmother with secret recipes from the old country?"

He gave her a half smile. "Sorry."

She shook her head. "It's a real shame. I liked that story."

"Yes."

They'd reached the porch and slowly took the steps, one at a time, until they were in front of the door.

"How did you find out?" she asked, turning to face him again.

His face took on a hooded look and he shoved his hands down into the pockets of his jacket. "I've got some friends in law enforcement. I made a few calls."

She looked at him, tilting her head. Was that a subtle hint that she and Carl had better watch their steps?

"What did your sources have to say about me?" she asked tartly.

He started to grin, then cut it short. "I'll let you know when I get the full report."

She reacted badly. That wasn't something she had wanted to hear. "You see this face?" she asked him, pointing at it. "Once again, this isn't adoring reverence for you. This is what we call anger. Anger and resentment and…"

His kiss stopped her words. He couldn't help it. It had to be done. Right now, she needed to be kissed, and he was the man to do it.

It was just a kiss. A kiss wasn't a surrender. It didn't mean he believed her. It didn't have anything to do with guilt or innocence. It was just an expression of desire, or maybe need, or maybe something even deeper. But that hardly mattered at all. It just was.

She gasped, her hands rising up to push him away, but they didn't try very hard. His mouth was hot and his arms were strong and she began to melt. And just as she began to enjoy it, he pulled away.

"Good night, Torie Sands," he said roughly, hunching deeper into his jacket. "Go to bed."

She felt slightly dizzy. "Where…where are you going?"

"I think I'll just take one more turn around the area. See what's shakin'." He gave her a quick grin as he turned to go. "See you tomorrow. Breakfast is at nine."

CHAPTER SIX

BREAKFAST was served on a wicker table on the terrace overlooking a clear blue ocean beneath a clear blue sky. It was a beautiful morning. Just what any real estate agent would have ordered if such a thing were possible.

Torie slipped into a chair beside Carl. He looked dreadful, like a man with a serious hangover.

"What's the verdict?" she murmured to him as she reached for a small glass of orange juice that was perched tantalizingly on a silver tray.

"The verdict?" he responded sharply, jumping as though the word startled him.

She looked at him impatiently. "What do you think of Shangri-La? Are you going to buy the place?"

"Buy the…? Oh, uh…" He moved restlessly in his chair. "I haven't seen enough yet," he muttered. Then he seemed to remember who she was and he frowned at her fiercely. "And you haven't been much help. You keep disappearing."

"You were the one disappearing last night," she said. "What were you looking for out there in the dark?"

He glared at her, then leaned closer to talk without being heard by others. "Look, way back when we first started talking about this, you told me you used to go with old man Huntington on his rock-hunting trips around the estate. Didn't you?"

She nodded carefully, wondering where he was going with this.

"And I asked you to draw up a map of all those places you used to go with him. His favorites. Didn't I?"

"Sure."

He glared. "You didn't put the caves on that map."

The caves. She should have known it would come back to the caves.

"Yes I did. I sketched in where they are along the coast."

"Vaguely. No detail. And when I went out there, I realized there was no way I was going to be able to search them." His nostrils flared. "They're like a maze. It must take forever to know where all the hiding places are in those caves. You didn't give me a clue."

She stared at him, wondering at the intensity she was seeing in his face. "You know Carl, maybe if you told me what you're looking for, I could help you better."

She stared at him. He stared back.

Come on, Carl, she thought silently. *Tell me you think you're going to find the Don Carlos Treasure. Admit it. Let's get it out in the open.*

He took a deep breath, his eyes smoldering with anger. She almost thought he'd heard what her mind was thinking.

"Just make a map of the caves," he said. "That's all I ask."

She smiled and waved as Lyla called out a good-morning greeting, walking out toward the edge of the terrace. Her smile faded as she realized where Lyla was headed. Marc was sitting on the broad stone wall, dangling his legs over the side. Lyla laughed as she kicked off her stiletto heels and prepared to join him.

Torie turned back to the man beside her, feeling a bit more grumpy than she had seconds before.

"Carl, I was a kid when I knew the caves that well. That was fifteen years ago. Do you really expect me to remember…?"

He leaned so close his hot, thick breath was on her cheek. "What were you doing down there yesterday?" he demanded. "What's in those caves?"

"Nothing," she said back, recoiling and frowning at him. "That isn't the only place I went. I walked up and down the beach, remembering things from my childhood and just enjoying seeing it all again. I walked past the boathouse and went into the canyon to the little redwood forest."

"Redwood forest? What redwood forest?" He pulled out the map and curled it open at one end. "You didn't put any redwood forest on here."

"I guess I forgot it," she said coolly. She'd had about enough of Carl and she welcomed the chance to throw him off the scent of the caves. "Here, let me fix that." She snatched up the map and opened it to the coast area, grabbing a pen and quickly drawing in a tree where the canyon should be. "There it is." She handed the map back to him. "Have yourself a ball," she told him caustically.

She started to gather her things with every intention of leaving Carl and going over to the stone wall to see what Marc and Lyla were doing, but it occurred to her that she ought to warn him.

She turned and looked at him, wondering how she could have let herself pretend this man was sane and safe. Anyone could have seen he was nothing but trouble—ugly trouble. And now she was stuck with him. She sighed, but resigned herself to a duty warning.

"You heard about the Greeks?"

"No." He glanced around and didn't see them. "What?"

"It appears they were not what they seemed." She gave a little cough of a laugh. "Just like us. Funny, no?"

He looked uneasy. "What are you talking about?"

She leaned close and spoke softly. "Marc has connections with local authorities. They have connections with the feds. He asked for a background check and got one. The Greeks are not even Greek, and they are out on their ears."

He stared. "Are you kidding me?"

She shrugged. "Would I kid about a thing like that?"

He rose, shoving his plate aside. "I've got to get out of here." He glanced at his watch. "Okay, I'll be back." He looked up and jabbed a finger in her direction. "And I want you to be available at noon." He glared at her fiercely. "You're going to lead me through the caves."

She swallowed hard. Something about his obvious burning anger was beginning to put her on edge. "I told Marge I would join the group in a hike along the cliff after breakfast. I don't know if we'll be back in time to…"

"Be back," he said coldly, almost snarling at her, his eyes suddenly looking very bloodshot. Reaching out, he gripped her upper arm painfully. "I'm going to need you. Understand?"

"Okay," she said a bit breathlessly. "Okay. Take it easy. I'll be here."

He nodded, obviously trying to get a grip on his emotions. "Good. I'll hold you to that." And then he turned away, walking quickly in the direction of the stairs and toward the rocky shoreline.

She rubbed her arm, watching him go. The man was beginning to scare her. She turned, planning to go to where Marc was, but he was gone. Lyla sat alone, swinging her legs over the side, and that was not an inviting scenario. Torie turned back toward the house. It was probably time to get ready for the hike.

* * *

An hour later, the hike was in full swing. Their little group was straggling toward the cliffs about half a mile from the house. Torie was walking behind Frank and Phoebe and wishing she knew where Marc had gone. She was on edge and conflicted and not sure what to do next.

She regretted allying herself with Carl. He was obviously some sort of underhanded crook, and she didn't want to be associated with him any longer. She knew it looked bad, that it made her look less than honest herself. What did Marc think? She was afraid she might just know.

Marc had been her crush from the time she was about ten years old. He'd never looked twice at her, except for various, vague incidents in their past. But on the whole, he didn't know she existed most of the time. But she certainly knew about him.

She'd watched him grow from a gawky but adorable teenager to a slender willow of a young man, strong and sharp, smart and quick, brave but restless. He'd gone off to join the military because he needed something in his life, needed to do something, be somebody. She'd only been fifteen the last time she'd seen him, but she'd known what he wanted to do and she'd understood his hunger for life. She'd felt a bit of an echo of it in her own heart at the time.

And now he'd come home, thicker, stronger, more wary of life and its challenges. He'd been through some things out there in the world, things he wasn't going to talk about. You could see it in his eyes. He didn't seem to trust anyone or anything anymore. It made you wonder what he'd seen, what had been done to him, what he'd had to do to others that he might regret. He was a man.

And when he'd kissed her, he'd been her dream come true. She'd gone up to her room and slipped into her bed and stared at the ceiling, and gone over it—feeling his mouth on hers again, catching her breath in a gasp of sensual excitement like she'd never felt before.

No. Sorry, world. Those embers were not dead after all. The smoldering excitement of Marc was very much alive in her heart and soul, and she knew it would be hard to smother it at this point. Hard—or maybe darn near impossible.

She shook herself to get rid of the dream and forced her focus back on the hike. Marge was calling out instructions.

"If you keep a sharp eye out, you may just

catch sight of sea otters hanging around that black rock you see there in the bay," she was calling back to everyone. "And up the beach a bit, you'll see sea lions basking in the morning sun."

Their group consisted of Phoebe and Frank, Lyla and the Texan and Torie herself. And, of course, Marge, their fearless leader.

It was a beautiful morning but Torie couldn't conjure up much interest in the scenery. She was wondering what Carl was getting into and if Marc was there to stop him. She should be there, too. What was she doing going on a nature hike when time was racing, running away from her? She needed to get back to the project at hand.

Last night hadn't done her much good, but it had clarified a few issues. She knew now that Carl wasn't interested in buying Shangri-La, never had been. What she didn't know was what he *was* after. Something, that was for sure. And he seemed pretty crazed about getting to his goal.

One of the first things she planned to do was to see if she could find some of the old employees, someone who might remember her father. She knew it wouldn't be easy. But surely someone knew someone. In order to get to a position to make any headway, she would have to get friendly with an employee.

The Greeks were crooks and they were gone. The Texan wanted to find evidence of gold-mine potential on the property. Marge wanted to get enough money to head for the Bahamas—maybe with Jimmy in tow. So what about Phoebe and Frank? Maybe they actually wanted to buy the property. Who knew?

Marc didn't want his ancestral home sold out from under him. Torie could understand that. And he didn't trust her, but he didn't hate her either. Would that change? Would he start to hate her once he knew….knew about the little bag of Spanish gold doubloons she had hidden in the lining of her suitcase? She shuddered and closed her eyes, stricken and breathless just thinking about it. She had to find the truth—find it before anyone found those doubloons.

The sea lions came into view. Barking nastily, they flopped their huge bodies on the warm sand and threatened each other with dire warnings of terrible sea-lion battles to come. The little tour gathered around the edge of the cliff and stared down at them, fascinated. There was nothing cuddly about these beasts.

"Take pictures," Marge advised. "But don't try to go down and get close to them. They're not friendly and just might hurt you if they get mad enough."

Lyla came to stand next to Torie as they watched the noisy animals complain about their lot in life.

"They remind me of some ladies I lunch with," Lyla said with a laugh. "Never happy." She turned to look at Torie. "So, are you and Carl ready to make a bid on this place?"

Torie laughed. That seemed so far from her reality now. "Not yet, I'm afraid. How about you?"

Lyla sighed. "I do love it." She arched one carefully painted eyebrow. "Now if the son came as part of the estate, I might do some serious thinking about it."

"You mean Marc?" Torie said, stunned at the thought. "I doubt he's for sale."

"Oh no, honey." Lyla was the one laughing now. "Everybody's for sale. You just have to find the right price."

She was still laughing as she started toward the other side of the area, as though she found Torie immensely naive and it really amused her. Torie bit her lower lip to keep from saying something mean, but the encounter didn't improve her mood.

The incessant barking of the seals was setting her nerves on edge. She turned away from the cliff, shading her eyes and looking back toward the house. As though summoned by her impatience, a large horse appeared, coming toward them.

She stood where she was, transfixed, staring at the approaching animal. And then it got close enough to make out the identity of the rider. Marc, of course.

Marc. She felt as though there was something glowing inside her. She knew he was coming for her. She stood where she was and waited.

"Oh look," Lyla cried, noticing him too and beginning to wave. "Marc's got a horse. Oh, I love riding! Marc! Over here!"

As he rode closer, his mother started yelling at him, but he didn't pay any attention to her. The horse was big and black, a beautiful mare, and he reined her in as he came near, making her walk softly up to where Torie was waiting.

She resisted the temptation to give Lyla a smile, but she had one for Marc.

"Come on," he said, leaning down and reaching for her hand. "I want to take you to the village. There's someone there you're going to want to talk to."

She reached up to meet him and he pulled her up in front of him, effortlessly. She slipped into place with hardly a wasted move. Marge was still yelling. She looked back and smiled at them all. And then they were off.

They rode along the edge of the cliff, the blue ocean on one side, the stand of tall, green eucalyptus trees on the other. Torie felt glorious. The wind was in her hair, Marc's hard, strong arm was around her, holding her in place, and the large, wonderful horse was beneath them. The whole scene was magical and she knew she would never forget it. If nothing else, she would always have this.

When she saw the village ahead, she knew the magic would be fading, and she regretted it. If only they could always ride like this…on and on and into the night. This felt like something she'd been born for.

She leaned back and his face was there, near her ear.

"You want to go down by the beach before we go to the village?" he asked her.

She sighed and nodded. "Yes," she told him. "Let's do it."

There was a dirt road down the hill and then a paved road that came in and led to a boat-launching area. The beach was deserted. Sea gulls dove at them, then retreated to a nearby buoy to call at them from a safe distance.

She slid down off the horse and he swung down after her. They stood side by side, staring out to where the waves crashed outside the breakwater.

"Why is the movement of water so mesmerizing?" she asked him.

"I don't know." He turned to look at her, eyes hooded. "Maybe something in us wants to return to the sea."

There was a sense of danger in his gaze that disturbed her and she looked back toward the water.

"When I was a little girl," she told him after a moment of silence, "I loved *The Little Mermaid* movie. I would wander around, leaning against the furniture and looking lovesick, singing the Ariel song until everyone around me went mad with it." She laughed softly, remembering. "They were threatening to tape my mouth shut if I didn't cease and desist."

He grinned, looking at her sideways. He remembered hearing her singing in the old days. That must have been why she'd sounded so familiar when she'd sung in the fog. "Don't tell me you actually caved in."

She gave him a look of pure cheek. "What? You think I'm a complete narcissist?"

"No. I think you're stubborn as hell though."

She laughed and turned toward him, but he was frowning as he studied her face. "You know, I'm starting to remember more about you," he said. "You were around more than I remembered at first."

"Or more than you noticed at the time."

"Was that it?" He shrugged as though he wasn't convinced. "I know one thing. When I reached down for you at the cliff, and you took my hand and vaulted up in front of me on the horse, I suddenly realized we'd done that before."

Her eyes widened. Now he was bringing up things she'd forgotten herself. "Oh. Yes! That time I was walking home from the village…"

"And you found a lost dog—a little white one."

"With the sweetest little black nose." She grinned. "I was trying to carry him back with me but I had a bag of groceries I'd picked up for my mother and I kept dropping things."

He nodded, his blue eyes filled with humor. "I must have been about sixteen."

"And I was about eleven."

"I was riding Brown Sugar, my favorite Indian pony. I passed you and I think I said 'hi.'"

"Hah!" She gave him a mock glare. "You didn't say a word."

He frowned. "I must have said 'hey.'"

"No you didn't. You were much too cool to deign to speak to a little girl like I was."

He looked at her for a long moment, then sighed. "I think you're wrong," he said, slightly grumpy. "Anyway, I looked back and you dropped your brown paper sack and macaroni noodles went into the air like a bomb had been set off, and the little dog jumped out of your arms and began to bark its head off."

She winced. Some memories were just too painful. The sense of humiliation she'd felt that day came back to her in a wave.

"So I turned around. By the time I got back to you, you had it all back in your arms, but you looked like you were going to drop everything again any minute. I told you to give me the dog and the groceries."

"And I thought you were going to ride off with them and leave me there."

"But I didn't. I stashed the groceries in my pack and the little dog in my shirt, and then I reached down for your hand."

She laughed softly, staring off at the blue horizon. "And I felt like Cinderella," she said.

She remembered that feeling. As though the prince had asked her to dance. She'd been on cloud nine all the way home, even though she knew he wasn't exactly enjoying it as much as she was. Still, the most handsome boy she'd ever seen was being nice to her—for the moment. It made her whole summer brighter.

"I named him Snowcone," she mused. "I loved that little dog."

"Whatever happened to him?"

Her face clouded. "My father insisted on sending a notice to the paper and the real owners showed up three days later." She shook her head. "I begged him not to do it, but you know what my father was like. Strictly by the rules."

Marc looked at her speculatively and she raised her chin. She knew it sounded as though she was feeding him her vision of her father's character, but she didn't care. It was the truth. He might not know it, so she might as well let him in on it.

"Yeah," he said, then looked around to where they'd tied the horse. "I guess we ought to get going."

She nodded and followed him, still amazed and gratified that he'd remembered so much. There hadn't been many incidents between the two of them but what there were still shone like gold in her memory. She pulled her way up to ride in front of him again, wishing they could just head on down the beach. She closed her eyes and felt Marc's arm tighten around her.

But the ride slowed and finally came to a stop.

"We're here," he said, close to her ear, and she sat up straight and looked around.

The village had an old-fashioned, quaint look. Red-tile-roofed cottages were scattered all up and down the hills, most with flower gardens overflowing with blooms. Boats filled the small marina, many apparently working fishing trawlers. The business district boasted a coffee shop, a small market with bait shop, a real estate office and a rustic tavern with a wooden statue of an ancient mariner out front. The place looked about as it must have looked in the 1920s when it began as a tiny beach resort.

"You ready?" he asked her.

"Ready for what?" she asked, still floating in the mellow nature of the sunny day and only half interested in anything else.

"Ready to talk to Griswold."

She turned to look back at him. "Who?"

"Griswold. Don't you remember him? The chauffeur. He was there when it all went bad."

"Oh." She shivered and steadied herself. "Oh!" Griswold. Of course. He might have some answers. He was just exactly who she needed to talk to. She turned and smiled at Marc.

"Perfect," she said, starting to get excited. Then she looked at him in wonder. He really was going to help her. "Thanks. This is…really cool."

He laughed softly and shook his head, still holding her against himself as though he really didn't want to let her go. "Let's go see him before you get too appreciative," he warned. "You never know."

"Of course." She set her shoulders and tried to get tough. This was important. She couldn't be getting all silly over Marc and expect to maintain the sharp edge she was going to need if she was going to get anywhere.

They pulled in closer to the front of the tavern and dismounted. Marc tied the horse to a post at the entryway.

"Where did you get this nice horse?" she asked, stroking its velvet nose and getting a snuffle in return. She knew that Shangri-La didn't have any horses these days, though they'd had a well-stocked stable when she'd lived there before.

"I went down to visit with an old rancher down the road," he said, stopping to give the animal a pat as well. "Both his sons were friends of mine in high school and now they're both in the military. He's having trouble keeping his livestock exercised, so I volunteered to take this little lady out for a spin."

"She's a beauty," Torie agreed.

Two girls in tiny bikinis with beach towels thrown over their shoulders strolled by on their way to the sandy shore. They gave Marc the eye with youthful enthusiasm, making Torie laugh.

"Girls always did like you, didn't they?" she noted as they gave him a backwards look and disappeared around a corner.

He glared at her. "You think that's funny?" he challenged. "You try living with it. They're everywhere and they're a pain in the neck."

She laughed harder. "Poor baby. Such a burden."

He turned and glared at her, then paused as though really seeing her for the first time. A slow smile crept into his eyes. "I'm sure you get your share," he said.

Her laughter faded and she was suddenly uncomfortable. "Not me," she said, trying for a light tone that didn't quite work. "I'm not the type."

"Baloney."

A new warmth had come into his gaze and it was heating up her cheeks.

"You're not very self-aware, are you?" he said as he finished up securing the horse.

Now she was embarrassed and blushing crimson—but not in a bad way. She'd never considered herself a beauty and she knew in her heart of hearts that she wasn't. At least she never had been before. She was pretty enough on a good day. But she didn't have a face that turned heads. And yet something in Marc's eyes was telling her that she did, and suddenly, she was walking on air.

He smiled and gestured toward the tavern. "Shall we go in?"

She turned looked at the door, just a bit

hesitant. "How do you know Griswold is in here?"

"From what they tell me, he's always in here."

He took her hand in his and she took a deep breath. This could be it. This could be where she finally learned the truth of what had happened all that time ago. She looked up at Marc. He gave her a wink and she smiled. Time to face her father's past as if it were her own. She lifted her chin and walked in.

CHAPTER SEVEN

MARC let Torie go ahead and followed a few steps behind. This was her show, her quest. He wasn't even sure why he was supporting her this way. She said she was here to find out what really happened fifteen years ago, whether her father was unfairly accused, whether he shouldn't have been fired. If that was true, if that was really her goal, she was basically trying to prove his family's actions wrong—maybe even illegitimate.

And where would that take them all? Did she think she could find the truth—or maybe even the treasure—somewhere and show them all her father had been slandered?

Not likely. Insurance investigators and the police had both taken their turns at searching for the gold. And then, through the years, treasure hunters had come sneaking onto the property to try their own methods. No one had found anything yet. As far as he was concerned, that treasure was at the bottom of the sea. His father's goodbye note had said that was what he was going to do with it. Why did everyone keep trying to find something that just wasn't there?

Torie was only the latest, and she said her search had a new twist. Was she lying? Was the treasure really all she wanted, just like everybody else? He was pretty sure that was what Carl was after. And she'd come with the man, so it all fit together.

And yet, he didn't want to believe she was lying to him.

He groaned softly, hearing himself and hating his own weakness. He knew all about lying and being lied to. He'd been through it often enough to consider it a normal part of human relationships. Why would Torie be any different?

As they walked into the dimly lit tavern, he glanced about the room. People were scattered around at tables and along the bar, mostly men. There was one stocky, blond young man who waved, but he didn't recognize him. There didn't seem to be anyone there that he knew.

Torie was still flushed from his compliments a few minutes earlier and looking prettier than ever. He had to grin as he noticed one man after another stealing a glance her way. And true to form, she didn't see it at all.

And then he saw the man they were after, sitting at a corner table, looking as if he'd staked a claim to it long ago and wasn't going to give it up for love or money. He pointed him out to Torie and they made their way there.

Griswold was drunk. There was no getting around it. He was a pale, boney shadow of the dapper man he'd once been. He gazed up at Torie with bleary eyes and didn't have a clue who she was, even after she told him. Jarvis Sands was a name that seemed to spark some recognition.

"Jarvis? Jarvis? You mean, the butler at Shangri-La? Sure. What about him?"

"Do you remember him? Do you remember what happened?"

He frowned at her. "I should have had his job, you know. They only made me chauffeur because the lady wanted to swan around in front of her friends. They didn't need me. All I did was wash cars all day." He shook his head. "No. I don't remember nothin'."

"How about the Don Carlos Treasure disappearing? You must remember that."

He was frowning and it wasn't apparent whether he had actually heard her question. "He told me not to go, but I went anyway," he said sadly. "I went and he was right. I shouldn't have gone."

"Who? My father?"

He looked around as though he felt trapped and Marc reached out to pull her away.

"It's not much use," he said quietly. "He's in no shape to talk. From what I hear, he never is. If he ever knew anything at all, it's probably lost to history by now."

She nodded reluctantly. She was bitterly frustrated. Somehow she'd been counting on finding employees from those days and now that she'd found one, he was useless.

"You know, its sort of crazy," she said to Marc as they were leaving. "Almost everyone from that generation is either dead or ruined in some way. It doesn't seem right."

"Anecdotal," he muttered as he led her out. "Don't let life depress you. There are plenty of good things to think about."

She looked up into his face and shook her head, still disappointed, but vaguely amused. "*You're* giving happy-talk advice? Now I've seen everything."

"I have my happy moments," he protested. "I even get optimistic sometimes."

"But not for long, I'll bet," she said dryly.

They were outside by now and they both noticed the blond man from inside the tavern had come out and was leaning against a huge black Harley. He waved as they approached, then straightened and came toward them.

"You don't remember me?" he said, smiling in a friendly fashion.

Torie gasped. "Is it Billy Darnell?" she cried.

He nodded. "You got it."

Torie reached out and grasped his hand in hers. "You remember Billy," she said over her shoulder to Marc. "Alice was his mother. The cook at the estate back in our younger days."

"That's me," Billy said, looking pleased.

"It's so good to see you! How's your mother?"

"She's fine. She lives down in LA now. She likes being close to my sister and her family."

"Of course." Torie thought quickly, going over the past. Billy was a year younger than she was. Being children of the Shangri-La staff, they'd spent some time together, though they'd never been particularly close. But when you were eleven and twelve and there was no one else around to hang with, you made do.

"Billy and I used to go on day-long mineral-collecting trips with your father," she told Marc. "We would trek out along the cliff at dawn, backpacks full of drinks, snacks and lunches, and your father would lead us to the most interesting places, nooks and crannies that you would never think existed if you just drove by them. And he'd find some quartz or some rocks with hornblende or muscovite and he'd use his rock hammer to break specimen-sized pieces out of the rock. Then Billy and I would wrap them in paper and pack them away in canvas bags and then tote the bags home for him." She grinned at Billy. "We had a glorious time."

"That we did," Billy said, grinning right back.

Marc nodded at the reminder and listened to them reminisce, but the whole thing created a bit of an empty feeling in his soul. He'd known his father was interested in rock collecting, but he'd never really paid much attention. He'd only listened with impatience whenever his father tried to talk to him about it. Which might have been why he never got invited along on any of these expeditions. Probably because he was too old when the hobby began to appeal to his dad. He'd been seventeen when Torie was twelve.

Still, he wished he'd known, wished he'd participated. It seemed more and more that there was a whole side to his father that he had known nothing about. He would have been a good man to get to know.

Too late now. He grimaced. He wasn't used to feeling this sort of regret. It made him uncomfortable. He looked at Torie, and for some reason, he felt a little better. She was like a light into the past that he'd been ignoring for years. She was helping him clear up some things. For the first time, he realized he was actually glad she'd come back to Shangri-La.

Torie brought up the treasure and Marc began to listen more carefully. Billy remembered it, but he claimed he didn't know anything about what had happened to it, other than the newspaper accounts about Hunt having dumped it in the sea, and didn't think anyone else knew anything new about it either.

"There's really no one else still left around who was working at the place in those days," Billy said earnestly. "Except Griswold, of course. But he's not much use these days."

They chatted for a few more minutes, and then Torie gave Billy a hug and they said good-bye. He rode off on his motorcycle; they got back on the horse.

"I'll drop you at the house," Marc told her. "I've got to get this little lady back home before she starts to worry about lunchtime."

She smiled, liking that he had a sense of understanding for a horse. Okay, it was time to admit it. Down deep, she knew him well enough to know he was a pretty good guy. Unless something had changed him while he was overseas, he was one of the best men she'd ever known. Maybe his family had been cruel to her father—he hadn't been involved. Not directly anyway.

Closing her eyes and letting the sway of the ride take her, she mused on life and the U-turns she seemed to find all along the way. So far, it had been a disappointing day as far as her aims and goals were concerned. What if she never found out the truth about her father? What if the truth was hidden somewhere and no one alive knew where it was? Could she live with that? Could she go back home and find a way to be happy? Could her mother snap out of the depressive state she'd been in for years?

Not likely.

Even more scary, what if she found out the truth and it was worse than she'd ever believed? What if her father was really and truly guilty? What if there was even more to it, more things he had done? Her mind cringed away from those stray thoughts. Some ideas were just too painful to explore.

Too soon, Shangri-La loomed on the hill ahead. She remembered she'd told Carl she would be back in time to go over the map with him again. That hadn't happened. The time had long passed. He was going to be angry.

Oh well.

She turned back to look at Marc.

"Can I come with you to your neighbor's?" she asked him. "I don't want to go back to the house just yet."

He nodded, his face unreadable. "Sure," was all he said.

But he didn't complain when she leaned back against him. He was strong and warm and she had a sudden fantasy of letting him be her champion in the world. She could use one. The only problem was, she had a feeling he wasn't in the market for a girl like her. After all, she tried to get his attention before, when she was a chubby young adolescent. That hadn't worked out so well.

Now she was back and he only cared because she was threatening his family's reputation with her crazy theories and searches.

But at least he was paying attention now. She smiled at the irony of it all.

"How can big things happen—big, important things that change the shape of our lives—and a few years later no one remembers anything about them?" she asked him over her shoulder.

He didn't answer for a long moment. Finally he leaned forward and spoke softly in her ear. "The people who are directly affected remember. Sometimes it takes a surprise to get them to open up to the past once they've tried to put it behind them. But they remember when they have to."

She wasn't sure she bought that. It seemed as though her father had passed through this life without anyone much noticing him. He'd tried so hard to be a good man and good at his chosen profession—and he'd done well at both. But when his heart got broken, so did his spirit—which started the chain of tragedy that pretty much ruined her whole family. And no one seemed to care.

If only the treasure had never disappeared. If only they had stayed and she'd finished her childhood here where she belonged. He would still be alive today, and her mother wouldn't be the faded shell of a woman that she was. Everything would have been so different.

She glanced back at Marc. His father might still be alive, too. And Ricky? She didn't really know what had happened there and Marc definitely bristled whenever she asked questions.

If only she could pretend she was any closer to finding out about her father. She'd always had a feeling deep in her heart that clearing his name would change everything. It wouldn't bring any of those people back to life, of course, but it would surely brighten her mother's life—and her own.

Funny, but in some ways she had begun to realize that she felt close to Marc. He was a part of her past. She might even venture to call him a part of her present. There was a reserve in him that appealed to her.

And then she frowned, wondering if it was really just a certain dignity that set him apart—or was it actually a wariness, and a basic distrust of her and who she was.

They delivered the horse to the neighbor and got into Marc's long, low sports car. She expected him to turn for home, but instead, he took a side road that took them on a curvy two lanes into the hills. He pulled into an overlook and turned off the engine.

"Wildflowers," he said by way of explanation.

She looked out and sighed. "Wow. How beautiful."

The hills were covered with masses of golden California poppies fighting for space with sky-blue lupine and bright yellow mustard, all dancing in the breezes. In the distance, looking back at the way they'd come, she could see the blue ocean. Oaks and flowering purple bushes filled the valleys. It was one of the most beautiful places she'd ever seen.

They got out and walked to the edge of the overlook, leaning against the guardrail that had been put up for just that purpose. She breathed in the beauty, but all the while, she couldn't ignore the sense of presence in the man beside her.

She finally turned and smiled at him. He didn't smile back, but his eyes were warm and she was beginning to think they might have a tender moment, if she played her cards right. Her heart began to thump a bit harder.

And then he pulled her right back into the maelstrom.

"Have you decided what it is that Carl's looking for yet?" he asked her.

Carl. Her shoulders sagged and she felt a pang of guilt. He must be wondering where she was. But she knew he would want more than simple work on the map. He was going to insist she come with him to the caves and show him what she knew. She wanted to avoid this at all costs.

"Uh…no," she responded evasively. "Why? What's your theory?"

He shrugged and looked out at the hills. "I think he's after the same thing most people who come nosing around here are after: the Don Carlos Treasure."

"But…" She hesitated, biting her lip. This was what really bothered her. "I thought your father sent it to the bottom of the sea when he sailed out that awful day. Wasn't that the story? And then his boat capsized and he… he…"

"He went down with the treasure. At least, that was what his suicide note said he was planning to do."

"Is there really any proof that he took the treasure out there with him? Does anyone know for sure if it's really down there?"

He didn't answer. She watched as his handsome face turned to granite. Reaching out, she touched his arm.

"I'm sorry, Marc. I know it brings up unhappy memories to talk about it."

He turned and stared down at her. "If we don't talk about it, we'll never get to the truth. And this may surprise you, but I want the truth as much as you do."

She searched his eyes. Was that really true? What do you know? Just as he had decided that, she was becoming more ambivalent. What if the truth only made things worse?

But Marc seemed to be transitioning into a philosophical mood. He leaned out over the railing and looked toward the ocean in the distance and went on, almost as though to himself.

"You know, I hadn't thought about it all, the whole situation, for a long time. Years. I was sort of blocking it out." He glanced sideways at her. "There were a lot of people at the time who asked the same questions you just asked. How did we know the treasure was truly gone? We had people coming here in droves, sneaking onto the property, digging up the rose garden, moving logs around, trying their best to find out where he'd actually hidden the treasure. It was like the California gold rush all over again."

"How awful." She glanced away, wondering if he looked at her as one of those scavengers. Why not? In a way, she was like them. Only she already had a part of the treasure. He just didn't know about that, and she hoped she was going to leave without him finding out. What she was after was the explanation. That was all.

"It didn't let up for a long time. Marge was always calling the police, and then there would be a confrontation. I didn't have to deal with it, since I was overseas. But I sure heard a lot about it."

"From Marge?"

"Yeah. She wanted to sell from the beginning. I kept trying to talk her out of it."

"But she kept things going around here."

He nodded. "I've got to give her that one. She did okay for a good long while. She kept writing me about these great offers she was getting, and then they always fell through. After awhile, she gave up. I hadn't heard from her about selling for about five years now." He ran his fingers through his thick, dark hair. "But this time she's determined. This time, she's going to sell."

"And this time, you want to stop her."

He was silent and she stood beside him, so close and yet so far. She could feel that he hated this, that he didn't want his family estate going to strangers. She wasn't sure how finding out the truth about the treasure would help him deal with that. A part of her wished she knew a way to help him. There was nothing she could do.

"So you're not in the military anymore," she said, more to fill the silence than to find out anything new.

"Not really. But when you've been in as long as I have, a part of you will always be in there. It gets in your blood."

She nodded. That made sense to her. The military could be a pretty intense experience, one that changed many people forever. She looked at him candidly. "What are you going to do with the rest of your life?"

He laughed, leaning back with both elbows on the railing. "That's what I like about you, Torie," he said, his gaze ranging over her in a way that made her tingle. "You don't play games and beat around the bush. If you want to know something, you just ask."

She gave him a quick smile. "You, on the

other hand, try to change the subject and don't give straight answers."

"You want an answer? Here goes." He took a deep breath and gazed off at the horizon. "I got experience in a lot of things in the service. Security, business management, electronics, diplomacy, espionage." He looked at her. "I even filled in as a wedding and bar mitzvah singer from time to time."

"You're kidding." The picture that conjured up made her laugh out loud.

"No," he protested, half laughing himself. "I was pretty popular at it."

"I'll bet." She could see the young girls swooning now.

He rolled his eyes at her amusement, but he went on.

"So when I got out, I started looking around at opportunities. But my mind kept going back to Shangri-La."

"Of course," she murmured. Her mind did too. All the time.

"I started wanting to come home. The more I thought about it, the more it seemed to pull at me." He turned to look at her more closely.

"You know, this is a wonderful place. There are a lot of options right here on the land. My grandfather made his fortune as a breeder of racehorses. My father spent a few years developing a world-class vineyard, selling his grapes to the best wineries along the coast."

"I remember that."

He looked at her, one eyebrow raised. "What do you think of me putting in a winery right here?"

"It would take a lot of start-up money, wouldn't it?"

He nodded. "Yes, it would." He shrugged and the faraway expression was back in his eyes. "Aw, what the heck. No point living in dreamland. Marge is going to sell, come hell or high water. She's got that look of determination in her eyes. She wants out of here. And I don't have the resources to stop her."

There it was again, that note of pain the tore at her when she heard it. "Will she give you a part of the proceeds if she does sell?"

"Why would she do that?"

She shrugged. "Maybe because you're like a son to her. Stranger things…"

His laugh was short and cold. "Not Marge. She wants to take the money and run. And she really doesn't owe me anything. She's the lonely widow. I'm the ne'er-do-well stepson. Never those minds shall meet."

"It just seems…"

"Community property," he said shortly, pulling himself upright and starting back toward the car. "I'm not a part of that."

She followed behind, kicking her feet into the dirt. "It doesn't seem fair."

"My only claims are emotional and courts don't much care." He turned to look at her. "Besides. I'm a grown-up. I should be making my own way in the world."

She stared at him, suddenly realizing that he was as much stymied by Shangri-La as she was. She couldn't move on with her life because these unanswered questions haunted her.

And he was no better. He couldn't stop loving Shangri-La, even though he had no hope of ever running the place as his father had done, and his grandfather and all the Huntingtons before that right into the days when Spaniards roamed these hills and tall ships cruised the coast.

They were a pair, lost and lonely, wandering in the wilderness, looking for a home.

"Making your own way is one thing," she said softly. "Losing your home is another."

They'd reached the car. He pulled her door open and held it. She appraised his tousled hair, his clear blue eyes, his incredible handsomeness, and she felt a surge of emotion. Was it affection? Or the sense that they were kindred souls who ought to join forces to fight the darkness? Whatever it was, the impulse took hold and she went on her toes, threw her arms around his neck, and kissed him on the mouth.

"Thanks, Marc Huntington," she told him, smiling at his startled look as she stepped away again. "Thanks for helping me get home that day with Snowcone in my arms. Thanks for being here to help me now."

"Anytime," he murmured.

But he didn't reach out and pull her into his arms as she had secretly hoped he would do, and his eyes were hooded, giving no hint at what he thought about what she'd done.

They rode in silence all the way back to Shangri-La, but she didn't regret that kiss.

The group was lounging sleepily on the patio furniture arranged casually on the terrace, enjoying the scenery. The sound of the surf in the distance, the cries of seagulls, the platoons of dignified pelicans swooping past—all very seductive selling points for Marge.

Torie hurried past, giving them all a wave

after she noted that her fake "husband" wasn't with them.

Marge glanced up and scowled. "Where've you been?" she demanded.

Torie stared right back. "Out," she said with an artificial smile. "Looking for facts. Looking for truth."

"Truth," Marge said in mock disgust, but she was looking more sharply at Torie, as if she was beginning to see something familiar about her. "Good luck finding any of that in this world," she muttered.

Torie turned her back and headed for the stairs, wondering what it would be like to get that woman in a small room with third-degree lights shining in her lying eyes. It wouldn't hurt to have a few grizzled old investigators to help her crack the woman's defenses. She smiled to herself.

"Oh, Carl said to tell you he was exploring the caves again," Lyla called after her.

"Thanks," she called back, taking the stairs quickly. And then she paused, looking at Carl's closed door. If he was out at the caves, this was a perfect opportunity to take a look at what he might have in his bedroom.

Should she? Why not.

After all, she was looking for facts, wasn't

she? And Carl was looking for something else. She had a feeling she knew what that something was, but it would be good to confirm it. And anyway, she wanted to know what he was up to.

She looked up and down the hallway. There was no one coming. Quietly, she slipped into the room.

Carl seemed to be a very neat man. No discarded clothing littered the floor. Nothing was hung on the chair. His suitcase was closed and propped against the desk. Papers were stacked neatly on the nightstand and she looked through them quickly. They seemed to be old insurance claims and she didn't see anything interesting on them. The corner of his briefcase was barely visible under the bed and she pulled it out and opened it. Inside was a sheath of newspaper clippings. The first one to catch her eye bore the headline: Gold Doubloons Show Up Along the Central Coast.

Gold doubloons. That was what the Don Carlos Treasure had been mainly made up of. She snatched the clipping, stuffed it under her shirt, and prepared to leave. The last thing she wanted was to be found sneaking around in Carl's room. Just the thought gave her the shivers.

And that was the moment she heard footsteps coming down the hall toward where she was.

CHAPTER EIGHT

TORIE'S heart began to hammer and her breath seemed to be stuck in her throat. She glanced around the room, zeroing in on the closet, the only place where she might hide in. But if she got caught in there, it would be ten times worse than just hanging out as though she was waiting for him.

Quickly, she sat down on the bed and stared at the door. If he came in, she would have a story ready. "Where's that map?" she would say. "I thought it might be here so I could work on it."

He wouldn't believe her, but at least she'd have a cover story.

The footsteps paused, as though someone was about to knock. She bit her lip and held her breath. A shriek of laughter came from downstairs and someone called. She couldn't tell who it was or what they were saying, but it seemed to get to her visitor. He—or she—

seemed to turn, and the steps went back toward the stairs. She let her breath out slowly, listening intently.

She then slipped out again and into her own room, where she threw herself down on the bed and tried to regulate her breathing and calm her pulse. That had not been a fun few minutes she'd just gone through. She didn't want that to happen again. That probably wasn't Carl who'd stopped at the door and then left. Whoever it was would likely be back though.

She pulled the article she'd stolen out from under her shirt and looked at it. She had to show this to Marc.

But she needed to get cleaned up first. Rising from the bed, she pulled off her rumpled clothes and put on a fresh pair of designer jeans and a soft blue sweater. Then she stopped to take a closer look at the article.

It was dated nine years before and seemed to have been printed in a county newspaper. Gold Doubloons Show Up along the Central Coast. The article claimed that a stash of the ancient coins must have been found lately, since coin dealers were reporting that people from the area were selling them in numbers that hadn't been seen for years.

"Nine years ago?" she muttered, frowning. How could that have any impact on today? She should have taken more of the articles. Too late now. She wasn't going back there.

Folding the article, she stuck it into a pocket of her jeans, then turned to look at where she'd stowed her suitcase under the bed. Reaching down, she pulled it out, found her key and unlocked it. With her hand, she felt along the lining. It was still there—the little bag of Spanish gold.

Her heart started pounding again. Could it really be a part of the treasure? What else could it be? And why had she found it among her mother's possessions just a few weeks before?

She shook her head. "Daddy, Daddy, what did you do?" she whispered to herself. Then she closed the suitcase and put it back under the bed, pushing it far enough back so that no one would notice where it was unless they were down on their hands and knees, looking for it. She couldn't really think of more she could do.

With a heartfelt sigh, she started downstairs. Detouring into the kitchen, she snagged a sandwich on her way out. Suddenly, she was ravenous.

At the doorway, she looked down on the little party on the terrace. Marge and the Texan were having a loud argument. Phoebe and Frank seemed to be taking sides—against each other. Lyla was pouting and playing up to Jimmy. Somehow she had to get past this nightmare bunch and find Marc again.

"Hey, you," came a half whisper from across the hall.

She whirled, and there he was, just coming out of the library.

"This way," he said with a jerk of his head. She followed him to a small French door at the end of the sitting room. A moment later they were slinking down a garden path and into the eucalyptus trees.

"You read my mind," she told him. "I was not looking forward to joining that group."

"You're wise beyond your years," he said, glancing back toward the house. Then he looked back at her, his blue eyes sparkling. "Have you ever been to the car barn?"

She had not, though she remembered hearing about it years before. The car barn had been Ricky's domain and Ricky's hobby was race-car driving.

"Never," she said.

"Until now," he told her. "Let's go."

It was a long walk and they weren't in any hurry. Stone benches had been set out here and there many years ago. They spent the next fifteen minutes remembering other times they'd been this way.

"The trees weren't quite so thick then," she recalled, looking up at the tall redwoods around their path. "You could see the ocean from here."

He nodded. "I remember when you could see the whole coastline from here, all the way down to the caves and up to the village."

"I wonder if Carl is back from the caves," Torie mused. Then memories of the newspaper article popped into her head. "Oh! I've got something to show you."

She pulled out the clipping. "What do you think of this?"

They stopped and sat on a nearby bench. He read the whole thing before he said a word.

"So where did this come from?"

She couldn't avoid the guilty look her face took on. "I took it from Carl's room. He had a stack of them, and some old insurance papers in a folder."

"And this is all you got?"

She nodded. "I just snatched it up and ran like a rat."

He gazed at her for a long moment, then shrugged.

"I remember this," he said. "I wasn't here, but a friend sent me this article when it first came out." He shook his head as though dismissing the importance of the clipping. "I thought at the time that either someone had a fertile imagination or a new stash of doubloons had been found."

He looked into her eyes and she frowned. Somehow his show of earnest common sense was ringing false with her. Was he trying to con her for some reason?

"Shangri-La isn't the only large estate along the coast you know," he said somewhat defensively. "There are plenty of cave networks too, along with hidden canyons. Back in the eighteenth and nineteenth centuries, the Spanish were all up and down this coast. I'm sure there were many places that were used for hiding various treasures, and I'm sure most people who find them keep it pretty quiet."

"But they have to let others know when they go to coin brokers to try to cash in," she noted.

He nodded. "Sure. And that doesn't happen very often. Mostly, people would rather keep the treasure for themselves. To people like my father, the historical value is more important than the cash you could get for it."

Was that understandable? Maybe. "Where did the Don Carlos Treasure originally come from?"

"My grandfather, William Canford Huntington. He found it in the thirties. He was trying to map the caves and ended up breaking down a ledge to be able to reach further in. Behind that ledge he found a pile of gold doubloons and other coins, along with some jewels. The bag they had been in had been eaten away, but the coins were bright and shiny as they'd ever been." He smiled, remembering the stories he'd heard. "But you must have seen it. My father had it in the display case in the library for years."

She shook her head. "I don't think I ever saw it."

"It was right in the house all the time I was growing up."

"That must have been quite an exotic display. But I never went into your house. I wasn't a guest, you know." She blinked with mock innocence. "Just a humble servant's child."

He rolled his eyes and groaned.

"It was stupid, of course, to have it just sitting there. It should have been in a security deposit box at the bank. But you can't show it off if it's not there."

"Ah, vanity."

"Vanity and greed."

He rose and held out his hand to pull her up. She took it, looking into his face to see if he'd had any new thoughts about her.

Just checking, she told herself. But she was disappointed once again. The man just didn't feel the things for her she felt for him. *Pity.*

And then they reached the car barn. She never would have found it on her own. It was a large, echoing warehouse-sized garage built into the side of a hill. The entry consisted of a set of huge double doors, but they were impossible to make out in the gloomy forest area. Weeds and vines covered it and years and years of branches and leaves and sifted dirt had been built up against it by the wind and rain. Luckily, Marc remembered where it was supposed to be and once he found it, the two of them worked for a good twenty minutes at removing debris before they were able to pull the doors open.

"God only knows what we're going to find in here," Marc said as he cleared a path for her. Before going in, he found the fuse box and threw a breaker, making sure they would have lights inside.

What they found when they went in was amazing. The door seemed to have kept the place hermetically sealed and it was like stepping back into past times. The inside was probably as clean as it had been when Ricky had last been working there. There were six bays, four of them filled with cars. Two of the cars were elegant models from the twenties or thirties, one restored and the other in the process of being so, both beautiful reminders of a bygone age.

"This one's an Auburn Boattail," Marc told her proudly. "I helped Rick with it a lot. It's beautiful, isn't it?"

"Gorgeous. Like something from an old movie."

He nodded. "The other's an old Mercedes. Both these cars were my grandfather's. When he realized how good Ricky was with cars, he gave them to him, along with this place. Ricky spent all his time here. In fact, most of the time over those last few years I think he lived here."

Opening a side door, he revealed a small room with a cot and some bedding.

"Ricky's apartment," he said with a smile.

"He even had a small cook stove and a lot of supplies over there in the cabinets."

"And an ancient microwave," she noted, pointing it out.

"Right. I can just imagine the gourmet feasts he was able to serve up in this place." Marc's eyes had a faraway look. "Ricky and I were never real close. But he was my brother. And I miss him."

His voice cracked just a little bit in the last sentence and he made an impatient move, as though he could erase it. She had a lump in her throat. She was finding herself in tune with him more and more, feeling what he was feeling. Or at least, trying to. Maybe she ought to cut it out. Before she knew it, she was going to get herself in too deep.

She tried to remember Ricky. He was taller and thinner than Marc, and a few years older. He always seemed preoccupied and she had the feeling he never really saw her at all. She was invisible as far as he was concerned. He was always thinking about cars and he obviously had zero interest in younger kids of any type. She never took it personally.

Not the way she took Marc's lack of interest. His hurt.

"I think my father came out here to see

what Ricky was working on," she said slowly, thinking back. "I remember him talking about it. I think he liked Ricky a lot."

He nodded.

"Marc, what happened to Ricky? How did he…?"

A spasm of pain crossed his face, but only briefly. "What would you guess?" he said shortly. He waved toward the other two cars, a souped-up Mustang and something else she didn't recognize that was also kitted out. "Amateur race car driver dies in crash. Some make it to the pro level, others die trying."

His voice was bitter. She glanced at him quickly, but he turned away.

"At least he was doing what he loved," she tried tentatively.

He swung back and glared at her. "That's supposed to make me feel better? People say it every time and it doesn't help anything at all. It's so lame."

She winced. He was absolutely right. "I'm sorry. I was just trying…"

Now *her* voice was breaking and he groaned and reached for her, pulling her in close and burying his face in her hair. "I'm the one who's sorry," he said gruffly. "You're a sweetheart and I don't need to be yelling at you."

She raised her face. It felt so good in his arms and she wanted to stay there forever. Was he going to kiss her this time? There had been so many chances and he'd passed them all by. She wanted to taste him so badly. Couldn't he read that in her eyes?

He looked down. There was something smoky in his gaze, something sensual, an awareness and a sudden flash of something that might be desire. She caught her breath and yearned toward him. He leaned closer, his lips almost there.

And then his face clouded and he seemed to pull himself back with a jerk, even pulling his hands from her shoulders. Turning, he walked toward the cars.

She closed her eyes and drew in a deep, deep breath. When would she ever learn?

They spent some time looking at the cars and he told her a bit about them. Fifteen years had passed since Ricky'd left them here, and they were hardly even dusty.

"It almost feels as though he might walk in that door any minute," Marc said. "Everything looks so much the same."

She nodded. "I'm glad you brought me

here," she told him. "I'm glad to know more about your brother. The picture is more complete that way."

Marc was rummaging around in a cabinet. "Hey, look at this," he said, pulling out a wine bottle. "From the Alegre Winery. Bottled in 1994. Made with our grapes."

She laughed. "If only we had some wineglasses."

He produced them with a flourish out of the same cabinet. There was even a corkscrew. He started to open the bottle, then looked around.

"We can't just drink it here on the floor of a working garage," he said. "We need a little elegance."

The Mercedes from the 1930s had that in spades. He opened the door, pulled forward the back of the passenger seat, and escorted her into the beautifully upholstered back seat, then went around to the driver's side and slipped in beside her, bottle and glasses in hand.

The crimson wine poured into the crystal glasses and sparks of light and color flew around the room. Torie raised her glass and he met hers with his. They clinked, looking into each other's eyes. Suddenly there was an air of excitement trembling in the atmosphere.

"To Shangri-La," she said. "And all it's glory."

"To truth," he countered. "And to us finding it soon."

She bit her lip. She didn't want to think about that right now. She was here in a beautiful, luxurious car, the sort of car rich people drove to mansions in the old days, the kind of car movie stars stepped out of to begin their walk on the red carpet in front of movie premiers. She could smell the leather, see the gleaming paneled wood, feel the soft seating, and here in her hand was a gorgeous glass of wine.

But best of all, she was in touching distance of the man she had always been almost in love with. It was a magic moment and she didn't want to waste it on painful subjects.

Sipping the wine, she let the bite of it warm her throat and she smiled at him. She wasn't a drinker. This was going to go to her head right away. She ought to be careful.

"More?" he asked, holding up the bottle.

"Lovely," she answered, surprised to see that her glass was empty. She'd never had wine so delicious before. And she seemed to be thirsty.

They talked softly for a few minutes, going

over their day, their ride to the village, their stop to view the wildflowers. She told him about a friend who ran marathons and he told her about a friend who raised Siamese cats. Their bottle was empty, but he produced another.

And then he told her, looking deep into her eyes, "You know what your biggest problem is?"

The fact that you won't kiss me? But she couldn't say that aloud, even though the wine was making her feel giggly.

"No," she said, melting in the thrill of his gaze. "Why don't you tell me?"

He suddenly seemed very wise. "You trust too much."

She reared back, not sure she liked that. "In what way?" she asked carefully.

He looked at her as though trying to decide something. Finally, he reached out, cupping her chin in his large hand, as though he meant to study her face, and she let him, though her heart was fluttering in her chest like a lost bird. When he finally finished his thorough observation, she sighed as he drew away again.

"You trust Carl to bring you here, even though he's probably a crook," he said quietly. "You trust things people tell you as long as they're nice about it." His mouth curled in a wistful smile. "Worst of all, you trust me."

"I do not," she said stoutly.

He grinned. "Yes you do."

She blinked rapidly. "Well, at least I give people a chance. You don't give anyone the benefit of the doubt. You don't trust anyone, do you?"

His eyes narrowed. "Trust is for suckers."

She drew back, frowning. "That's a horrible attitude."

He shook his head as though she just didn't understand, and he took her hand in his.

"Let me tell you a little story. Something short and sweet. Something that will give you the picture of the world I live in, and why I think trust is overrated."

She smiled, her fingers curling around his. For some reason what he'd just said seemed so very amusing. "Lay it on me, baby," she said, leaning toward him.

A look of alarm came over his handsome face. "Hey. How much have you had of that stuff?"

She giggled. "Sorry. I was just trying to get in the mood."

Moving with calm deliberation, he took the glass from her hand and put it out of reach.

"See, this is what I mean. If you were smart, you would be very wary of what I might do if you get a little tipsy."

"Don't worry," she said bravely. "I've got all my wits about me. Such as they are." She laughed out loud.

He gave her a baleful look, but he settled back and continued his cautionary tale. "Okay. This happened years ago, when I was young and still a nice guy."

"Unlike today." She nodded wisely.

He frowned his disapproval of her chattiness. "Unlike today," he allowed. "I was in South East Asia. The country doesn't matter. But I was on a mission. A pretty dangerous situation. And I fell in love."

Now he had her complete attention.

"Oh," she said softly.

"The area was beautiful. White-sand beaches. Sweet, friendly people. My mission was to extract something important from the desk of a local plantation owner. My job was to get in and get out. Under no circumstances was I to interfere with local customs or get involved in local affairs. No roiling the waters."

She nodded to show she understood completely. "And I'm sure you did a very good job of it, didn't you?"

He stared at her for a moment, then laughed softly. He touched her cheek, looking at her as though he enjoyed the view. "Yes, darling. I always did a good job. But right now I'm talking about the girl I fell in love with."

"Oh." She felt so sad all of a sudden and she wasn't sure why.

His face took on a faraway look.

"She was so beautiful, so tiny, so fragile, like a flower. I was pretty young and I fell like a ton of bricks. She enchanted me. She told me how her family had sold her to the plantation owner because they were desperately poor. They had eight other children to feed. She was one too many."

"How terrible."

"Yes. The plantation owner had promised to take good care of her, but he'd lied. She was so unhappy. She told me whispered tales of how cruel he was."

He shook his head, remembering his naive reaction. "I was outraged. I burned to protect her. I couldn't get her out of my mind. So I did something very stupid."

"Uh-oh."

"Yes. Uh-oh. You see, when my mission was complete, I took her with me."

She'd known he would end up being the hero. "Good for you."

"No. Not really." He grimaced. "We travelled for two days and finally reached the city and I got us a hotel room. I had so many plans in my head. I thought…" He stopped, looked at her and his mouth curved in a bitter smile. "Hell, what does it matter what I thought? I woke up at dawn the next day and she was gone. And so was all my money."

She gasped. "Oops."

He looked at her and started to laugh. "It's like you've got an alter ego just waiting inside you," he noted. "She can only come out to play when you drink. Is that how it is?"

"I don't know what you're talking about," she said very primly, sitting up straight like a good girl.

He laughed again, then shook his head. She looked like an angel, her blond hair flying like gold threads around her face, her green eyes sparkling, her eyelids heavy with the effects of the wine. The need to kiss her came over him like an urgent wave, choking him for a moment. He had to look away and breathe hard a few times to get himself back on track.

"Okay, I'll wrap this story up. The beautiful girl I thought I was in love with not only stole all my money, she fingered me to the local crime gang. I got away from them, but I took a little memento with me."

Pulling up his shirt, he showed her the scar.

"See?" he said as she gasped, wide-eyed, at the ugly wound that contorted his beautiful skin just below his rib cage. "That's what you get when you trust someone."

Reaching out, she put her warm hand over the damage. And then, without thinking, she leaned down and pressed her lips to it.

As he felt the heat radiating from her mouth, he sucked in his breath, then reached to pull her up.

"Torie, you'd better not…"

She ended up in his arms and all his determination not to touch her melted away like April snow. What had he been saying? It was gone. All he could think about was her warm, wonderful body against his and her hot, tempting mouth so close.

He kissed her. He felt a twinge of guilt. After all, she might not be doing this if it weren't for the wine. But it was too late to use that as a reason to pull away. He was kissing her and she was the most delicious thing he'd ever had.

She sighed and bent back as though offering him something more than a gesture. Something in that move hit him directly in his natural male response center.

Desire bloomed in him like a small explosion. He wanted her. He wanted his mouth on hers and his tongue exploring her heat, and he was getting that. But he needed more, and the need was beginning to grow in a way he wasn't going to be able to control. He had to hold her hard against him and he had to touch her breasts and make her cry out so that it would make him even more crazy and… and…

He had to stop. It was becoming obvious that she wasn't going to stop him and he'd counted on that. He'd have to do it himself.

"Torie." He tried to pull back.

She whimpered when his mouth left hers and she reached with her warm, provoking hands to slide against his skin and lure him back.

"Torie."

"No," she whispered, flattening against him. "No, don't leave me."

"Torie, we have to stop."

"No." She shook her head, her eyes tightly closed, as though that would make his common-sense thoughts go away.

"Yes, Torie. We have to stop."

She still pressed against him, her face to his chest. Her sigh was deep and heartfelt and he began to stroke her hair. In moments, she was asleep.

He held her there, taking in her fresh scent and her soft feel. An emotion swept through him and he wasn't sure he knew exactly what it was—but it touched his heart. He knew that. A part of it contained a tug on his sensual responses, but there was more. He felt the warmth of affection, the strength of protectiveness, and he couldn't stop looking at her and how pretty she was.

Still, it was all crazy. He'd been in love and it never came to anything good. It usually meant a certain type of heartbreak. It had been a good five years since he'd even chanced it, and he'd vowed never to let it happen again. So he was okay. He was protected, inoculated against the disease. He wasn't going to worry about it.

But he was going to enjoy this. This, he could handle.

So he sat there and held her and waited for

her to wake up. And he thought about his situation.

Why was he here? What exactly did he want out of all this? He wanted to save Shangri-La. That was it. He wanted his home to stay in the family. And since he was the only real Huntington left, that meant he wanted to keep it himself.

He'd tried to talk to Marge about him becoming caretaker while she went off and did what she felt she had to do, but she didn't want to hear about it. Marge wanted money. She wanted enough cash in hand to leave the country and live on for the rest of her life. If she could get that from any of these people she had gathered here, she would be gone like a flash. And he just didn't have that kind of a bankroll.

So what were his options? Few and far between—not to mention, weak. If the fortune-hunter crowd was right and the Don Carlos Treasure was hiding on the estate somewhere, things would be different. But he didn't believe that for a minute. His father's suicide note had been stark and emphatic. He thought the treasure was cursed and he wanted it at the bottom of the sea. Marc had no doubt his father had done what he said he would do.

So why was he helping Torie? Why was he letting her dream? Maybe because her dreams connected with his own in an odd way. She wanted to prove her father didn't steal the treasure. He wanted to know what had actually happened. She wanted to clear her father, he wanted to exonerate his own. And maybe help to fix something that had haunted his family—if it could be fixed.

And that was why he wanted to help her find the journal. Who knew? There might be something written in there that could clear up a lot of questions—and put some ghosts to rest.

But that was a pretty slim thread to put his hopes on and he didn't really expect anything even if the journal was found.

He looked down at Torie's pretty face, her lashes making long shadows on her cheeks as she slept. He had to smile. To think that chubby little girl throwing apple cores on his car had grown up to be something like this— and possibly his only hope at getting to the truth. That made his grin wider.

Still, he wasn't sure about her. There was a huge element of distrust in his gnarled soul. He'd been lied to one too many times. He didn't trust anyone and, if he was honest with himself, he had to admit she hadn't proved herself at all. She'd just become so appealing to him that he was willing to give her a pass—for now.

Wasn't that it?

CHAPTER NINE

TORIE was somewhat surprised to wake up alone in the back seat of an ancient luxury car, but she stretched and yawned and smiled. She was still a little fuzzy in the head, but she knew that something good had happened. And then she remembered what it was and she sat up straighter and sighed happily. Now the only problem would be if Marc regretted it.

She wondered where he was, but then she heard someone rummaging around in the storage room at the end of the hall and she assumed it was him. She sighed. There wasn't much point in sitting here waiting for him to come back as though she was hoping for a rerun. Something told her that wasn't going to happen.

She ran her fingers over the leather seat and turned to look at the beautiful dashboard with its hand-rubbed mahogany trim. They just didn't make them like this anymore. There

was even a long shelf just under the dashboard, running the width of the car. Ladies
probably stored their long kid gloves there
after the party was over. She smiled at the
thought, and then her gaze sharpened. There
was something pushed far back into the shelf.
You could hardly see it but when she bent
low, she could just make it out. It looked like
a small notebook of some kind. Maybe the
sort of thing people wrote their mileage down
in. Or…

Her heart began to beat like crazy and her
breath choked in her throat. A journal? Her father's journal? She pushed forward to the front
seat and leaned to reach for it. And at just that
moment, Marc came back into the room.

"Hey sleepyhead," he said, carrying a couple of cans of car wax in and stowing them
away on a shelf.

She jerked back, pulling her hand in and
turning scarlet. "Oh, uh…hi."

He grinned at her, probably thinking her
pink cheeks were the result of her thinking
about the snuggle they'd shared. But that was
just as well, because she suddenly realized she
wasn't going to tell him what she'd just seen.
If it turned out to be the journal, she wanted a
little time to see what it had in it. Who knew

what sorts of things her father might reveal in something like that?

"Find something?" he asked curiously.

"No. No." She shook her head and tried to smile.

"I've been out looking through the shelves." He gestured toward the storage room. "I didn't find anything either."

She gazed at him out the car window. "Thanks for letting me take a little nap," she said cheerfully. "I hate to be a girl who can't hold her liquor, but better to sleep than to do something crazy."

He grinned again. "Oh, I don't know. Crazy can be good too."

She gave him a look and laughed, and he turned back to the storage room, disappearing in through the door.

She reached out quickly and grabbed the little notebook, and then her hands began to tremble.

Her father's little leather journal. His name was embossed on the front cover in gold— Jarvis Sands. And inside was the handwriting she knew so well. She flipped through it quickly. There was someone else's handwriting on the last few pages. She only had to read a couple of lines to realize it had to be Marc's father who had added his thoughts.

But Marc was coming back. She could hear him approaching the doorway. Quickly, she closed the journal and jammed it down deep into the back pocket of her jeans.

She had the grace to flush again as he came out and smiled at her. The guilt made her look and feel nervous. But he would just think she was still shaky over what they had shared. She wasn't going to show the journal to him until she knew for sure what it revealed. She just couldn't see any way around it.

A few minutes later, they left the car barn and walked out to the cliff that overlooked the ocean. The sun was low in the sky. The people back at the house would be preparing for dinner about now. They were going to have to decide what they were going to do.

But not yet. For now, they found a fallen tree and sat on it while they watched the sun move toward a sunset. He made no move to get closer, and she knew instinctively that he wasn't planning to kiss her again. Did he regret doing that earlier? Who knew? It made her a little sad to think that he might. Still, there was nothing she could do about it now.

"What a beautiful view," she said softly.

He nodded. "Think of being a local Native American in the nineteenth century and watching Spanish galleons come sliding into the harbor," he said. "We had an archeologist doing a paper on this area one year. He found evidence that lots of ships stopped along this part of the coast. Can't you just picture how that would have been?"

Yes, she could picture it. She'd lived her Spanish-era fantasies on her own on the beaches and in the caves from early on. Such a great place for a child to grow in.

Tears filled her eyes and she blinked hard, angry with herself for letting it get to her again. She stared out at the ocean, throwing her head back to feel the wind in her hair. She was filled with sadness and a wave of nostalgia. She'd been so happy here as a child—despite any latent insecurities. The mood in the fresh ocean air was filled with peace and a sense of well-being. Life had been like that here—right up until the day her father had been accused of stealing.

That was the dividing line. Everything had begun to fall apart on that day and it had only gotten worse since.

She'd had good times with friends and success in her job. She couldn't claim it had been all angst and torture since her fifteenth year. But her father's agony had been a dark cloud over her family.

His eventual suicide and her mother's breakdown had only made things worse. She felt as though her heart and soul were restless, looking for answers, aching for closure. Could she ever find happiness without knowing? It felt to her as though that would be impossible.

Rising, she rose and walked out to the edge of the cliff, looking down at the rocks below. Then she turned to watch Marc in the gathering gloom.

"So tell me this," she said. "What was the official story? What did you hear at the time? What do most people around here believe happened?"

He looked back at her coolly. "About what?"

Her eyes narrowed. "About when my father was fired."

He sighed. It was pretty plain he didn't really want to go over it. But he did.

"Okay. Here's how I remember it. I was in premed at UCC, living with a couple of friends in an apartment off campus. It was a Sunday, late at night. My father called to tell me the Don Carlos Treasure had gone missing."

"Wait. What were the circumstances?" Walking back, she sat beside him again. She wanted to be sure she got this right. She might never have another chance.

"Circumstances?" He shrugged and thought back. "I'm not sure."

"Here's what I remember," she said. "And believe me, I've gone over this in my mind a thousand times. My family and I had been gone that weekend. We were up in Monterey to see the aquarium. Your father was at some geology lecture in Los Angeles and your mother was off on a trip with friends. Palm Springs or somewhere like that. Ricky was at a comic-book convention in Oregon."

He shook his head, his gaze hooded. "I don't remember all that, but you were there. I wasn't."

"That's just it. None of us were there. When we got home, no one else was back yet. Even the rest of the staff was gone. No one else was due back until Monday morning. But about an hour later, my father went up to the house to get back to work. Even though he didn't have to." She almost rolled her eyes. "He always had that darn sense of responsibility toward the place—and toward your father. He wanted everything perfect for when Mr. Huntington got home."

Marc nodded and almost smiled. "That is how I remember him. I know my father had a lot of affection for him at the time."

She nodded too. "Your father got back unexpectedly about eight. My father went out and met him on the drive. He told him the treasure was missing. He'd gone into the library and saw that the display case was empty. He'd been searching for the last hour, in a panic, hoping someone had just moved it. Your father rushed in and they both spent rest of the evening searching."

Marc frowned. "Didn't they call the police?"

She shook her head. "My father came home about midnight and told us what had happened. He said Mr. Huntington didn't want to call them until he'd talked to everyone, just to make sure someone hadn't borrowed it and was bringing it back. He didn't want to start a scandal."

He stared at her. "Any idea who he had in mind?"

She held his gaze for a long moment before she answered. "No." She sighed. "The next day, after everyone was back, the police were called. They questioned everyone. And someone accused my father."

Marc looked at her sharply. "Just because he was the one who was alone in the house at the pertinent time?"

She hesitated. She'd run out of proven facts. Now she was going to venture into specula-tion. "I think someone gave them more to go on than that. Someone made some things up about my father. Someone who had a reason to need the money and might have stolen the treasure themselves."

"Need the money," he repeated softly. "So now you've got a motive."

"Maybe."

They were both silent for a few minutes, and then Marc spoke, his tone emotionless. "My family was having lots of money prob-lems fifteen years ago. Did you know that?"

"I...no, not really." To tell the truth, that shocked her.

"Mostly tax issues as I remember it. I had to work full time in college. Marge had to give up some renovation plans she had because we didn't have the money for it. My father had some property in Hawaii and he sold that. We were scraping the bottom of the barrel for a while there."

"I didn't realize that."

He considered, then turned to look into her eyes. "You don't suspect me."

She waved that away. "Of course not."

"Or my father."

"No."

"Or the cook, or Griswold, or any of the staff."

She shrugged. "There doesn't seem to be any backing to suspect any of them."

He raised an eyebrow. "Ricky?"

"Ricky?" She was shocked at the thought. "No, of course not."

He knew the name of the person she suspected, but he set that aside. "What about a random theft? A burglar? Someone from the village?"

She shrugged. "Always a possibility."

He nodded. "And then there's the obvious one." He took a deep breath before he said it. "How about your father?"

She winced. "That was what they decided. A few days later, they arrested him. They took him up to the county detention center." Her voice trembled as she remembered. "It was horrible."

"Yes."

She took a deep breath, wishing she could

blot out the memories of that time. "He claimed innocence. My mother fell apart. I had to withdraw from my school and stay home to take care of her." She shook her head, holding it together. "I don't think she ever recovered. Not really."

"I'm sorry, Torie." He looked at her, then away, raking fingers through his thick hair. "I feel a bit cut off from all this. I wasn't there, didn't know all the details. I wish I'd been more involved."

She threw out her hands, palms up. "You were away at school. You couldn't help it."

"The next thing I heard," he said, "was that the treasure had been found buried in the caves. Right where the Spaniards had put it in the beginning." He shook his head. "Seems odd, doesn't it?"

"Yes." She tried to steady her voice. "There still was no hard proof my father was involved. The police found the treasure, and he was released right after that. But…" She shrugged helplessly. "He was fired anyway. And still under a cloud."

Marc grimaced and looked out toward the ocean.

"You'd think once the treasure was found,

they could have at least given him a chance," she murmured.

"Be realistic, Torie," he said a bit firmly. Then he seemed to regret his tone. He turned toward her. "Actually, my father considered your father a good friend as well as the best butler he ever had. I'm sure he tried to find a way to keep him on. I think there were others who counseled that he had to go."

Her voice hardened. "You mean Marge."

He hesitated, then coughed and looked away. "When it came to Marge, I'm afraid my father didn't seem to have much of a defense on anything."

She took a deep breath, knowing she was going to sound bitter, but determined to let it out anyway. "So because he couldn't stand up to Marge, we were thrown like refugees into the street."

His head went back and he frowned at her, but he tried to keep his tone light. "Hardly. I'm sure you drove off in a car."

She shook her head. "You know what I mean."

"I know what you mean, and I know it was painful. Unfair, too. But things in life are often unfair. Most people find a way to get over them."

She glared at him. She knew what he was saying was true, and his manner wasn't cold or lacking compassion, but these hard truths weren't what she wanted to hear right now.

"What else?" she asked shortly. "What did your father ever tell you about it all? What did he say about my father?"

Marc thought that one over for a few minutes, then raised his head and looked at her.

"My father didn't say anything about it when I came home that year. It was sort of the big unmentionable. Everyone tiptoed around it."

"Oh."

That obviously wasn't going to satisfy her. He sighed, threw her a rueful smile and dug a bit deeper.

"It wasn't until about a year later, when Ricky died that he talked to me about it. It was the night after the funeral. He'd had too much to drink and he couldn't stop crying. Neither could I. It was…pretty awful that night. But at one point, he started talking about the treasure. He said that maybe we should have left it in the caves in the first place. Maybe fate— or the ghost of Don Carlos—had tried to put it back where it belonged."

She shook her head. "I wish I could buy that."

"Yeah." He looked at her sideways. "At that point he had the treasure in a safety deposit box at the bank. No more display in the library case."

She nodded. "Did he say anything else?"

"Yes." He sighed and stretched out his arms. The sun was almost gone and it was starting to get cold. "Actually, he blamed all our troubles on that bag of gold. He thought it seemed like a curse on the family. Like nothing good had happened since the treasure was found and brought into the house." He glanced her way. "He went through the list. My mother dying. His marriage to Marge. The financial ruin he was facing. Having to fire your father. And then, Ricky."

She almost smiled. Despite everything, she felt a warm spot for Marc's dad. His heart had been in the right place most of the time. And she'd always known his marriage to Marge was a rough element in his life.

It was tempting to find a way to blame everything on Marge—but she knew that was the easy way out. She wanted to know the truth, not just something that might be true to make herself feel better.

Rising again, she walked to the cliff and watched the sky turn red as the sun disappeared over the edge of the earth. It was always startling how quickly it began to disappear once it got that close.

"Why isn't there anyone who knows anything else?" she asked into the wind. "Why doesn't someone come forward? I just have this feeling..." Throwing out her arms, she turned back to face him.

"You know, I corresponded with local authorities quite a few times over the last year, trying to see what I could dredge up. But nobody tells me anything. All the people who work in law enforcement around here are young. They're all different from the ones who worked here then. No institutional memory at all."

He nodded. "The trail has grown cold."

"But how are we going to find out just what were the facts?" she cried, her frustration quivering in her voice. "Why did this happen?"

Marc moved impatiently. "Face it, Torie. You're never going to know it all. Some things just aren't knowable."

She stared at him. "You really are cynical, aren't you?"

He held her gaze with his own hard blue one. "I try to be."

She frowned at him fiercely. "So tell me, Marc. What do you think happened? Be honest. Was my father guilty? Tell me what you think."

Marc stared back at Torie's impassioned face. What did he think? Did he have to make a statement right now? Did she really need to know everything going on in his brain?

No. What good would it do her to know?

"Forget it, Torie," he said, rising to walk toward her. "I'm not going to play that game."

It wasn't until he got a few steps away that he realized tears were running down her face.

"Torie," he began, reaching for her, but she whirled and started off in the opposite direction as though she couldn't bear for him to see her crying.

"Torie, wait."

He went after her. She knew he was coming and she started to run. The next thing she knew, she'd tripped on a rock. She'd been moving fast and the momentum sent her sprawling at the rim of the cliff, suddenly half over the edge and sliding toward the rocks below.

"Torie!"

He had her in seconds, pulling her back up to safety. She clung to him, tears forgotten as she gasped for air and looked down at the disaster she could have fallen to.

"Oh my gosh! Oh, thank God you caught me."

I'll always catch you.

He held her tightly and swallowed hard. Had he really thought that? Good thing he hadn't said it aloud.

"Are you okay?" he said instead, letting her go enough to be able to get a good look at her.

"I don't think so," she admitted, flattening her hand on his chest. "My ankle feels like it's being stabbed."

He swore softly as he pulled her up in his arms and carried her back to the fallen log. Placing her carefully, he pulled off her tennis shoe and took a look at the ankle. It was swelling fast.

He looked up at her doubtfully. "I don't think you're going to be able to walk on it."

"Oh, sure I am. I've got to." She slid down and tried. "Ouch!"

He shook his head but a smile was creeping through. "You're cute," he told her, "but silly. You can't walk on that. I'm going to have to carry you back."

"Never!" she insisted.

Not again. That first time had almost done her in. But really, it wasn't her own peace of mind she was worried about. It was a long way back to the house and she was no lightweight, no matter what he said. Gallantry was all very well, but common sense was better.

"You did that once when we didn't have that far to go. You're talking about almost a mile here, and through some rougher terrain."

"No problem."

She held him off. "Listen to me. I happen to know you have a golf cart back at the house for running around on the estate."

He looked surprised. "You're right. I forgot about that." He hesitated, then shrugged. "But I'm not going to leave you out here waiting in the dark. Besides, I want to get you to a doctor as quickly as possible."

Her ankle was throbbing and she wanted to get back to the house and put an ice pack on it. She began to relent. Once she got back to her own room, she would have time to look through the journal and…

She reached back to feel for the journal, which was supposed to be in her back pocket. It wasn't there. Panic began to race through her blood. She looked at the area around the log, trying not to be too obvious. Nothing. Then toward the edge of the cliff where she'd fallen. There it was, lying out in plain sight. She looked at Marc quickly, hoping he wouldn't see it. But how was she going to get to it without him noticing? And how was she going to get to it at all with her ankle this way?

"I'm going to carry you back," he said decisively.

"But..." She tried hard to think of a way to stop him but nothing came to her. She was beginning to think she would have to leave it behind and come back later—only hoping that a squirrel didn't take it home for some light reading.

"Ready?"

"No, I..." Nothing popped into her mind. Nothing at all.

"Oh, wait," he said. "I wanted to take some of that car wax back with me. Think you can carry it for me?" he asked her.

She nodded, suddenly hopeful.

"Okay. I'll be right back." He went back into the car barn.

She rose quickly, gritting her teeth to hold back her cry of pain. She grabbed the journal and pushed it back into her back pocket, then made her way back to the log, sinking down just as Marc reappeared at the clearing.

"Okay, let's go," he said, handing her the car-wax cans.

She breathed a sigh of relief. He hadn't noticed a thing.

He swung her up into his arms and she clung to his neck with a sigh. If nothing else, this would be a great chance to hold on to him. She was beginning to think that very action could get to be a habit with her.

He started off through the forest. It was pretty dark now, and he had to watch his step. She clung closely and breathed in the scent of him, just this side of swooning.

"You all right?" he asked.

"Absolutely." She sighed.

"How's the ankle?"

"It hurts." She tested it and flinched. "Yes, it's not too good. You know, I hope this isn't going to inhibit my activities." She frowned. "I was thinking, maybe I ought to try to talk to Billy again. He seems to be the only one who has any links to anyone who might be useful."

He hesitated. "Well, that's fine," he said slowly, "but you do understand that Billy was lying, don't you?"

"Lying?" She looked into his face. "About what?"

"My father."

"What are you talking about? I was there, remember? I know he went rock hunting with us…."

"No, not that. About not knowing anything about the treasure and what happened to it himself."

She stared at him. "How do you know?"

He shrugged. "I've got some training in intelligence work, you know. And I could see his eyes flicker a certain telltale way when the subject came up."

She thought that over for a few seconds, then looked up again. "So you think he really knows something?"

"I know he does."

She moved restlessly. "Let's go back there tomorrow. Let's talk to him."

"No." He gently squeezed her against his chest. "Let's leave it alone. Let it simmer. See what comes out in the wash."

She frowned and felt pouty. "You're mixing your metaphors."

He grinned. "But you get the general idea I was trying to communicate, don't you?"

"Yes." She looked up at him, eyes flashing. "You don't trust many people, do you?"

His face went hard as stone. "I don't trust anybody."

"Even me?"

He looked down and paused, then with a half smile, he said, "Especially you."

"Why?" She felt a sense of outrage, and yet…

"You have all the reason in the world to lie to me. Your motivations are as clear as your pretty green eyes."

And that was exactly why she wasn't going to show him the journal until she'd read it herself. If he didn't trust her, she surely wasn't going to trust him. And that was that.

CHAPTER TEN

THE others were back sitting around the fire pit in the dark. The flames leaped high into the air, giving their faces an eerie quality.

"Do you see Carl?" Torie asked as she craned her neck to see them all.

"Yes," Marc answered. "He's there."

"Darn. I was hoping he would have given up and gone home by now."

"Listen," he said softly to her, pausing before they went in to greet the others. "I'm going to put you down by Carl. You keep him occupied. I've got to call the doctor, but as soon as I get that done, I want to go raid his room."

"What?" she cried, alarmed. "Oh no, I don't think you should do that."

"Sure I should. I want to see those insurance papers. I think they might be very interesting."

She frowned. "But I think he might be suspicious."

"Of course he is. That's why you'll sit down here by him and keep him from going up to his room while I'm in there."

"But…"

"It'll work, don't worry."

He carried her into the middle of the group. "Wounded soldier here," he announced. "I'm going in to call the doctor."

They all gathered around, everyone exclaiming over her and talking at once.

"It's just my ankle," Torie said. "It's really painful but I don't think it's life-threatening."

"Let me take a look," Lyla said, pushing through the others. "I used to work as a physician's assistant before I got married to my beloved departed husband. I might be able to call upon my lazy brain cells for some helpful memories of what to look for with these things."

"Oh," Torie said, surprised. "Thanks, Lyla. I'd appreciate it."

Marc gave her a wink and disappeared up the stairs.

"It certainly looks like a sprained ankle," Lyla said after manipulating it to moans of pain from Torie. "That means mostly ice and lots of rest are needed. If you've got some bandaging, I can wrap it up and make it almost usable for walking. Which you should keep to a minimum."

"That would be great," Torie said, truly grateful for the help from the woman.

Marge went bustling after bandages, Jimmy brought out some ice, and Lyla went in to wash her hands. Phoebe and Frank clucked over her injury, asking for details, then went inside as well. It was getting chilly. Torie was finally alone with Carl. He leaned close, his eyes bloodshot and angry.

"Do you want to explain to me what the hell is going on?"

"Carl, I…"

"I brought you here for a reason. You keep disappearing on me."

She got a chill from the fury in his eyes. She could see it throbbing at his temple. He was really upset.

"I know, Carl, but…"

"I didn't expect you to go chasing after hot young guys. I didn't realize you were that sort of girl."

She stiffened and glared at him. "I'm not 'that sort of girl' and you know it. I came to pretend to be your wife so you would have the sort of presence you might need to put in a bid on the property. Now I can see that you never planned to do any such thing. You lied to me."

"What do you care?"

"I care about being lied to. And I'm not going to help you."

"Oh yes you are," he said harshly. "Tomorrow will be the last chance. You're going to have to go with me."

"To do what?"

"Help me navigate the caves."

She gaped at him. "You may not have noticed, but I've sustained an injury. It's going to be kind of tough to make a hike to the caves with a sprained ankle."

He stared at her ankle. It was swelling up like a balloon, despite the bag of ice she'd encased it in. He started to swear, one ugly word after another, and then he surged out of his chair, turning toward the house—the house where Marc was probably going through his room right now.

"No, wait Carl," she cried, grabbing at his shirt to keep him there. "Wait. Come here. We need to talk."

"I'm done talking with you."

"No you're not. We need to work this out. Maybe we can…"

He ripped his shirt out of her hands and

backed away. "Draw me a good map of the caves," he snarled. "Do that and we can talk all you want to."

She knew he was headed upstairs and she had to stop him. If he caught Marc in his room, she didn't know what would happen.

She tested her foot. Stabbing pain shot through her ankle and up her calf. She gasped with it. Too much. She couldn't do it.

"Carl," she called after him. "Come back here."

He was almost to the stairs. "Why should I?" he called back. "What have you done for me?"

"I have to tell you something. Something private. Please. Come back."

He stared at her as though weighing the possibilities, then reluctantly walked back across the patio. She almost collapsed in relief, but she couldn't let up. She had to find a way to keep him here.

"Come here," she coaxed. "Closer. I can't shout this."

Finally he came close enough and her hand shot out again, fingers tangling quickly into the fabric of his shirt, holding tight. "Closer," she said again.

He looked down as though he was afraid

she was going a little crazy. "I'm as close as I'm gettin'," he said firmly.

She leaned and pulled him even closer, whether he wanted it or not, then hissed in his ear, "You're after the treasure, aren't you?"

He looked startled and tried to pull away, but she had him. He tried to peel away her fingers, but she clung on tightly, desperate to keep him from going upstairs to his room.

And then, Marc was back, and she sighed with relief. Her hand loosened on the shirt and she half collapsed into her seat.

"Hello, Carl," Marc said coolly as he approached them. "How are you doing?"

Carl grimaced and looked away. "I've been better," he grumbled.

"I'm sure you have." Marc's smile was humorless. He was carrying a folder of papers and he didn't try to hide it. Carl glanced at it and away, then did a double take and blanched. Marc's smile widened.

"Say, Carl." He gazed at him levelly. "You know, I don't think you ever said exactly what you do for a living."

"Who? Me?" Carl blinked at him nervously. "Uh, well, various things. I'm a businessman really. Mostly import-export stuff lately."

"Ever spent any time in the insurance game?" Marc asked him casually.

Carl stared. "Insurance game? What do you mean?"

"Ever work for an insurance company, Carl? Ever done any claims adjustment? Fraud investigation? Things like that?"

Carl seemed to pale. "Listen, my past work experience has nothing to do with anything. I'm not officially applying for anything here. It's none of your business."

Marc's smile was pleased. "Thanks, Carl. That's all I needed to know."

He handed Torie the folder and reached under her knees to swing her up into his arms. "Come on up to my room," he told her. "We're fixing it up as a sick bay for you. Lyla is going to tape your ankle up and then we'll see where we are."

Torie looked back at Carl as she was carried up the stairs. He was staring after them, mostly trying to see what Marc had in that folder Torie was holding. And he looked very worried.

She sighed and leaned against Marc's shoulder as they left the area where they would be seen by others. "Why are we going to your room? Wouldn't mine do just fine?"

"It would not." He paused and looked down at her face. "I've had some information from my friend. He left me a message. He said, and I quote, 'Carl's one of the bad guys. Nothing outstanding on him at this time, but I wouldn't leave him alone with the silverware.'"

That was an uncomfortable thing to find out about the man she'd been pretending to be married to. She shuddered, but kept up the good fight anyway. "And how does this effect me exactly?"

"He seems to have a reputation for treating women badly. I'm not going to risk it. I'm keeping you close."

"Oh." Her gaze flickered up to his face. "So you're telling me that you're a danger-free zone yourself?" she asked him archly.

He grinned. "Hell no. But I promise to keep the rough stuff curbed for now. Until you're well and can fight for yourself."

She smiled back. "Deal," she said.

He started down the hallway. She looked at his beautiful smooth skin and the way his hair barely curled around it. She had a sudden impulse to drop a long, slow kiss on the side of his neck, but she managed to hold it back.

"So are you going to tell me what you found in Carl's room?" she asked instead.

He flashed her a smile and kicked open the door to his room. "All in good time," he told her. "Right now, Lyla is here to bind up your ankle."

"Ah."

She looked around as he plopped her onto his king-sized bed and sure enough, there was Lyla with a Cheshire-cat grin, playing with her beads and looking truly entertained.

"So Marc tells me he's fixing this room up to be your recuperation center. How handy for him." She batted her long eyelashes his way. "And will you be staying here, too?"

"Of course." He openly laughed at her. "I have to keep an eye on her condition at all times." He shook his head. "Though it's really none of your business."

"Of course not. And yet, I have a feeling this innocent young woman might need an older, wiser friend to help guide her through the tangled thicket of the male attention I'm beginning to sense here. If you know what I mean."

Marc smiled, but dismissed her at the same time. "I know just what you mean. But I think we can do without it."

Lyla shrugged and looked at Torie. "Just keep it in mind. I'm here if you need me."

Torie smiled at her but she didn't know quite what she could say to that.

"Didn't you have a husband when you first got here?" Lyla noted, putting a double knot in her long string of glass beads and tossing the end of it over her shoulder, out of the way.

"You mean Carl?" Torie gave her a shaky smile. "That was just...well, that's inoperative now."

"Inoperative." Lyla laughed out loud. "I see. That explains the strange situation with the separate bedrooms. I did wonder about that."

Marc chuckled. He couldn't resist. "You see, Carl is a shy fellow—socially inept. He felt intimidated by all you real-estate sharks and he thought he might need Torie along for moral support."

"Ah. Perfectly understandable." By now Lyla had manipulated the foot and analyzed what she could of the injury to the ankle. She gave the skin a light massage, then prepared the elastic wrap. "It seems to be a nasty one, dear," she told Torie. "But I think we can wrap it tightly enough so that you can use it at about fifty percent tomorrow."

"Oh, I hope so."

Lyla looked up with a smile. "Big plans?" she asked with a smirk.

"No!" She gave the woman a look of pure annoyance. "It's just that I'd rather be able to walk than not."

"A universal desire, my dear."

Marc was laughing. "You are a sly one, Lyla."

She smiled at him, her black eyes glittering in the lamplight. "I try to be." She patted Torie's knee as she finished up. "Now take two pain pills and call me in the morning." She looked up at Marc. "Have you got something for her?"

He nodded. "Thanks, Lyla. I appreciate it."

"No problem. And don't forget to take her down to the clinic for X-rays." She looked from Marc to Torie and then back again, gave a small resigned shrug, and smiled wistfully. "Have fun, you two," she said, and she was gone.

Marc found a couple of pills and a glass of water and then he handed her her pajamas and her toothbrush.

"Oh," she said, looking at him with wide eyes. "You went into my room too."

He frowned at her tone. "Does that bother you?"

"No, of course not." But it did. He could see it on her face. He frowned. There was that sense again that she had something to hide.

He hated distrusting her, but she kept giving him cause.

Better to find out now than later, he reminded himself silently as he waited with his back turned for her to change out of her clothes. But when he turned back and looked at her, her cheeks pink, her smile irresistible, he pushed that aside.

He was going to trust her as far as it went. They were partners in this quest, at least for the moment.

"The only things I saw in your room were the pajamas I was looking for and your toothbrush," he told her. "Carl's room was a different story."

"You found the stack of papers I told you about?"

He nodded. "There were more clippings, anecdotes about gold doubloons turning up in this area during that same period years ago. And then there were the insurance records."

"On the Don Carlos Treasure?"

"Yes. Marge tried unsuccessfully to collect insurance on it a couple of times. And each time insurance agents and investigators came out and did a lot of digging."

"How did Carl get hold of that information?"

"You heard him. He practically panicked when I asked him if he worked for an insurance company. Obviously, he did. He might have seen some of the articles about the treasure and started rooting through the files, then decided to come on up and take a chance on finding it himself."

"That jerk! And here he had me believing he wanted to buy Shangri-La."

"That'll be the day."

She grew more somber. "Do you suppose any of them will buy it?" she asked him.

He shrugged. "Not if I can stop the sale," he told her.

She glanced at her jeans, draped across the back of a chair. She could just barely make out the outline of the journal in the back pocket. She was beginning to wonder if she would ever get a chance to take a real look at it. Right there in that little book were her father's words, and maybe the answers to her questions. She glanced at Marc. She should tell him she had it. She should show it to him.

But what if there was something in there that she wouldn't want him to see? What if her father had implicated himself in…something? She couldn't risk it. She had to read it first.

And then, if there was nothing that needed to be hidden, she would show it to him.

She watched him, wondering.

And he was smiling at her, his head cocked to the side. "How are you feeling?"

"Fine. Really, I'm okay."

He reached out and touched her cheek and the warmth in his eyes made her heart stop. "You better be," he said gruffly. "I'm counting on it."

That Marc Huntington would look at her with such affection hardly seemed real. After all those years of thinking of him as an unattainable dream, here he was, acting as though he really liked her. Tears welled in her eyes.

"Hey." He frowned. "What's the matter?"

"Nothing." She covered his hand with her own and tried to smile at him. "I'm just sort of wrung out, emotionally."

He searched her eyes, then nodded. "You're hungry," he said. "I've got something I've got to take care of, and then I'll be back with some soup for you. Okay?"

She nodded, wondering if she really dared to be this happy. "Okay."

He smiled and was gone, and she closed her eyes and tried to steady her heart. Here she was in Marc's bed. How had this happened?

She smiled and settled in among the pillows, feeling as though she were on a cloud.

And then she remembered the journal. She listened. No sound of anyone approaching. Sliding to the edge of the bed, she reached for her jeans and grabbed the journal, with only a couple of twinges of real pain. But she had what she needed and she sat back and began to flip through it.

By the time she heard Marc coming back, she'd read enough to know her father was no thief. He'd started writing in the journal months before the treasure disappeared, and most of his entries had nothing to do with it. He made occasional notes about things that had interested him, the weather, who came to visit, discussions he and Hunt had had about politics or history. And then came the treasure and his anguish over being accused of taking it. She knew her father and she could tell that he'd had no part in it. What a relief.

Still, that didn't explain the little bag of gold coins she had in her suitcase. Where had it come from? Why? The first time she'd known anything about it had been when she'd begun packing up her mother's things. It was an emotional time. She'd finally had to admit she couldn't take care of her mother by herself any longer. She needed institutional care.

She'd found a very nice nursing home that she could barely afford. In fact, she'd had to start working at an extra job at a local restaurant, organizing banquets and setting up celebration parties, just to make ends meet. It had broken her heart to have to tell her mother she was going to have to place her in the home. Her sweet, dear little mother had looked bewildered, but she hadn't complained. Still, Torie hated to do it and she'd done a lot of the packing with tears in her eyes.

She'd been filling boxes with her mother's old clothes when she'd found the bag of gold. She'd never seen the Don Carlos Treasure with her own eyes, but she knew right away this was the same sort of thing—only smaller. When she tried to ask her mother where it had come from, she'd only looked frightened and turned away, biting her lip.

Torie could only think that her father had somehow ended up with some of the treasure—but how? Why? And that had started her journey back toward Shangri-La. She had to know the truth.

She didn't have time to read any of what Marc's father had written down. His handwriting looked like hieroglyphics and she was afraid she was probably going to need Marc to translate it for her. His writings came from a much later time period, probably just before he'd gone out on the sailboat with the treasure. Had he found out the truth? Did he know just what had happened?

She still didn't know that, but she knew from the entries in the journal that her father hadn't been guilty in the original disappearance of the treasure. Nonetheless, she still needed more facts.

When she heard Marc coming, she quickly shoved the journal under her pillow. She knew she would show it to him soon, but not yet. She needed to read what *his* father had written on those last few pages. She had a feeling that would answer some of the questions she still had.

"Hey," Marc said as he entered, a bowl of soup in his hands. "I was afraid you might be asleep already."

"No." She took the soup gratefully. It smelled wonderful.

He watched her eat for a moment, looking restless, then grimaced and raked fingers through his short hair, making it stand up like spikes on top.

"Carl's gone," he said shortly.

"What?" She stared at him. "Where did he go? Why?"

His gaze darkened and she realized he'd been curious what her reaction would be. Surely he didn't still think she might be attached to the man. She frowned, disturbed by that thought and not sure how to tell him how wrong that was.

"I told him to get out. He's not here for what he claimed he came for. No reason to let him stay."

"Oh."

"Don't worry about how you're going to get home. I'll take you."

She blinked a few times, thinking all this over. "But if Carl's gone, I suppose I might as well go back to my room," she said.

He shook his head slowly, warmth coming back into his gaze. "Not a chance," he told her. "Now that I've got you here, I'm not going to let you go."

She laughed. She couldn't help herself. This was all so crazy. Somehow she had to assimilate this through-the-looking-glass present with the past she remembered and still had to live with. And that reminded her of something.

"Last night, didn't you bring my family photo album back from our attic adventure?" she asked him.

He nodded. "Ready to look at it?" he asked her.

Was she ready? It might not be easy and she was in a pretty emotional state as it was. She bit her lip and told herself to stop being a baby.

"If you've got it here, I'd love to."

"I've got it." He took it out of the closet and handed it to her. "Mind if I look at it, too?" he asked.

She smiled at him and he took that as an invitation to come in next to her on the bed. They leaned back against the pillows as they leafed through the album. There were pictures of her mother, looking young and happy in a way she hadn't been for years, and her father, tall and dignified, looking like a man you would put all your confidence in. How could anyone have thought he was a thief? Her heart swelled as she remembered how it had been.

And there she was as a shorter, rounder version of the current Victoria Sands. It made her laugh to see it.

Marc looked at the pictures and shook his head. "How did I miss the gorgeous creature you were preparing to turn into?" he teased her. "Good thing you came back. I needed to be hit on the head with this one."

She laughed and gazed up at him. He stopped smiling and leaned down to kiss her.

She opened to him, still amazed he might want her. He said such great things to her but she was scared to believe him. She couldn't let this go too far. She couldn't risk being loved and left behind. Too much good had already been snatched from her. She couldn't let it happen with him.

He pulled her up so that her body was molded to his and she sighed with shivering pleasure. He was so hard and strong it took her breath away. The thought of making love to this man sent her head spinning. But she felt it. As his tongue explored her mouth, as her hands explored his skin, she felt the small, aching sweetness of desire begin deep inside her.

She pulled back but he followed, turning so that he was half lying on top of her, and the tiny desire leaped into flame. She had to stop this now or she would be burned away with the fire.

"Marc," she whispered, but he didn't seem to hear her.

"Marc." She pushed hard against his chest. "Stop."

He groaned and rolled away, leaving her feeling empty and alone. She closed her eyes and tried to get her pulse rate down to normal.

And then he was back again, but this time sweetly, kissing her eyelids, touching her cheek.

"I'm sorry," he told her softly. "I didn't mean to scare you. Torie, listen to me. I would never, never hurt you. And if you ever want me to stop, tell me and I swear, I'll stop."

She smiled at him tremulously. "I didn't want you to stop," she admitted to him. "But we have to. We just can't…"

He nodded and took up her hand and kissed her fingers. "I know. You're right." He smiled and settled back beside her. "Okay. Just let me catch my breath."

She leaned her head against him, happier than she thought she'd ever been. Was she in love? What a question. She'd been in love with this man since she was about ten years old.

It took a few minutes, but they were back discussing their mutual problem very soon. They still needed to unravel the mystery that was the Don Carlos Treasure.

"You know, I was thinking," Marc said.

"My father sent me a long, rambling letter just before he died. He didn't tell me just what he was planning to do, but if I'd read between the lines, I think I would have realized something was up. And he told me a lot of things I didn't understand at the time." He made a face. "I wish I had that letter with me. I have a feeling it might clear up a lot of this."

She hesitated. That, along with the journal, might fill in all the blanks for both of them. "Do you still have it somewhere?"

"I hope so. I'll have to look for it."

She should show him the journal. Of course she should. It was time.

"Marc," she began, steeling herself for the inevitable. He wasn't going to be happy that she'd kept it from him this long.

But a knock on the door interrupted her.

"Marc, you want to come down to the library?" It was Jimmy's voice. "Your mother has something she wants to talk to you about."

Marc groaned, but he answered. "Sure. I'll be right down." He dropped a kiss on her lips and rolled off the bed. "You get some sleep," he told her. "Your eyes are so dark they look haunted. You need some rest."

She nodded, half sorry she couldn't get the issue of the journal over with, half relieved to have it wait a bit. "Okay." She smiled at him. "See you in the morning."

"Sleep tight," he said, pausing for a moment to look back at her. His look was full of mysterious things she couldn't quite identify, but she thought she saw a warm sense of affection and a strong thread of hot desire in those eyes. It curled her toes to see it and she held on to that feeling for a long time after he went out the door.

CHAPTER ELEVEN

When Torie woke up, sunlight was streaming through the room and Marc was coming in with a breakfast tray. "I've got coffee and eggs and toast and some news."

She stretched, feeling luxurious. "News first," she said. "Then we'll see if I can stomach breakfast."

"You're expecting it to be bad news?"

"Always," she admitted. "I always want to be prepared for that."

He set down the tray. "Well, it just happens that this time you are pretty much right." He looked straight at her. "The Texan has signed on the bottom line. He's buying the place."

"What?" she gasped. "Oh Marc, no!"

He turned away and she was sure he didn't want her to see how anguished he was over this. Or maybe just plain angry.

"What will you do?"

He turned back and she saw that her second

guess was the right one. He was mad. There was no way he was going to let this happen without a fight.

"I haven't worked that out yet," he told her, his voice carefully controlled. "The problem is, my friend checked him out and he's for real. No baggage in his background. And he's got the money."

"Oh."

He shrugged. "But there's got to be something…some way. I just haven't thought of it yet." He smiled at her. "And I've got you on my side. Right? Maybe together…" He shrugged again.

She reached for the journal. She didn't even think about it. It was way past time she should have shown it to him. She held it out without a word.

He stared at it, then reached to take it. Just as his hand closed around it, a knock came on the door.

Jimmy again. "Hey Marc? Somebody named Billy is here to see you. He says he needs to tell you something about your father that you should know."

Marc glanced at the door, then at Torie. "How long have you had this?" he asked her, his voice rough and gravelly, his eyes dark with sudden suspicions.

"Marc?" Jimmy called again. "You in there?"

"How long?" he asked again, his eyes all intensity.

"Since yesterday. I found it in the car after we had the wine."

His gaze darkened. "Have you read it all?"

"No. Just what my father wrote. Your father wrote in it, too. I didn't read that."

Marc gave her one last long look, then shoved the journal into his pocket and turned to the door.

"I'm coming," he said.

And this time he didn't look back.

Torie groaned and fell back against the pillows. It shouldn't have happened this way. Now he thought she was keeping things from him—and he was right. She had. But there were reasons.

She had to go down and explain. Sliding out of bed, she pulled off her pajamas and quickly put back on her jeans and sweater. Going into the adjoining bathroom, she freshened up and combed her hair.

Looking into the mirror, she saw a familiar face, but there was a new light shining in her eyes. Determination. She was beginning to understand that she had something within her reach, something important, something to fight for. Finding out the truth about her father and the past was important too, but this wasn't about the past. This was about the future—her future. She'd never thought she would find someone like Marc to love. And now....maybe she would. Maybe. As long as she didn't mess it up.

She'd barely stepped out of the bathroom when the bedroom door swung open and Carl stepped in, closing the door behind him with a snap.

She gasped, and two seconds later wished she'd screamed instead, but by then it was too late. He had her in a choke hold and something made of cold steel was jabbing against her back.

"Just shut up and do what I say," he hissed into her ear. "I've got a gun. You don't want to find out whether I'll use it or not. I'm at the end of the road here, baby. If I don't get what I want today, I might as well put this gun to my own head and pull the trigger. So don't think I'll hesitate to use it on you."

She tried to talk but his hold was so tight, she could barely breathe.

"Shut up. We're going out to the caves. You're going to show me where that treasure is or neither of us might come back."

"I can't…" she managed to grind out.

"I know. Your damn foot. Don't worry. I've got the golf cart at the back door. If we can get that far, we'll go all the way."

He yanked her toward the door and she tried to comply. She had to in order to keep from choking. He hurried her along the hallway, then down the stairs. She gazed around as much as she could with her head in his hammer-lock grip, but she didn't see anyone. A moment later, he thrust her into the golf cart and started it up, racing out down the hill and toward the beach. She sat back, gasping for air. He didn't have his hold on her any longer, but he did have a gun pointed her way. She stared at it, looking right down the barrel. She'd never been so scared in her life.

Marc went down the stairs and into the library with a dark scowl on his face. Every time he started to think he could trust Torie, she did something like this—hiding the damn journal from him.

Why? There didn't seem to be any point to it unless she was still trying to help Carl in some way. Maybe she felt like she owed him one. Who knew? But he didn't like it.

He stepped into the library, his gaze involuntarily going to the empty display case where the treasure used to be. And then he saw Billy waiting for him, looking nervous.

"Hey, Billy. What's up?"

"I've got something I need to tell you. I should have told you and Torie yesterday, but I wasn't sure…."

"Go ahead. I'm all ears."

Billy laughed shortly and moved jerkily. "I have to tell you the truth, man. I…I know what it's like to miss your father and…I just had to tell you the truth."

"What about, Billy?" Marc's voice was patient but only with effort. He wanted to shake the younger man and get him to hurry up and tell him what he had to say.

"About a week before your father…went out in the sailboat, he came to see me. I was still in high school, but I was planning to go to college in Oregon. He asked me how I was going to pay for that and I said I didn't know. Try to get a job on campus, I guess. Take out loans. Whatever." He looked down and shuffled his feet, then looked back up and smiled slowly. "When I told him I was going to study geology, because of all I'd learned from him on those rock-hunting trips, he was tickled. And he..." Billy's face contorted. "He gave me something he thought might help when the time came. But I wasn't supposed to do anything with it or tell anyone about it for at least five years."

Marc nodded. He knew where this was going. He'd already guessed at least a part of it. "How much did he give you?"

Billy shook his head. "It wasn't money. Exactly."

"I know. It was gold doubloons, wasn't it? Old Spanish treasure."

Billy looked guilt-stricken. "Yeah. A whole handful of them." He shook his head again. "They were worth a lot. I waited five years, like he said, and then..." He drew his breath in sharply. "Those coins pretty much paid my way through college."

Marc stared at him for a long moment, and then he smiled. "I'm glad. And thanks for telling me about that."

Billy hesitated. "Do you think they were part of the Don Carlos Treasure?"

Marc shrugged. "What do you think?"

Billy sighed, then spoke softly after looking around to make sure no one was in earshot. "I wasn't the only one, you know. He gave some to Griswold. And to my mother. And to a couple of other people who worked at the house over the years."

Marc groaned. No wonder the word got out that the doubloons were still being held on the property. He should have known.

He talked to Billy for a bit longer, then walked out with him toward where his motorcycle was parked. He heard the golf cart start up and looked back at the house casually, wondering who was using it. As it began to careen off toward the beach, he got a flash of the driver—and his passenger.

Carl. And he had Torie with him.

He stood frozen for a moment, trying to understand what this meant. Was Torie taking Carl out to the caves? Was she still that close to him that she would help him that way? No. He couldn't really believe that. And yet, hadn't she held out on him where the journal was concerned?

"Damn it, Torie," he muttered, clenching his hands into fists.

But what if Carl was taking her out there against her will? Either way, he had to stop it.

But how? He couldn't run fast enough to catch them. He whirled.

"Give me the keys to your bike," he ordered Billy. "Quick! I need to borrow it."

"What? Are you going to take it out into the sand?" Billy asked, horrified. "You can't do that."

"There's a compacted trail," he said. "Come on, man, I've got to get Torie away from that bastard."

"Oh. Well okay then." He handed over the keys and Marc ran for the bike, kick-starting it into a roar and taking off toward the caves. No matter what, he was going to make sure Torie was okay.

Torie tried to get her bearings. She still couldn't speak. It felt as though Carl had crushed her vocal chords. She looked ahead. The caves were coming into view. What was she going to do once they got there?

Her voice wasn't working but her mind was clear and focused. She'd known those caves well when she was a child and her visit two days before had reminded her of a lot. She didn't know of any current treasure hidden there, but she did know of a sort of secret area that you could only find if you were looking for it. If she could lure Carl into that, she knew how to get back out again and he wouldn't have a clue. That was it. That was what she would try to do.

The only sticking point was the gun. What if he shot her before she got him into the blind alley she planned to lead him to? What if he realized she was trying to trick him? Then she would be sunk. A shiver went down her spine and she glanced at the man beside her. His face was contorted with rage and hate. Just looking at him scared her. He might do anything at any moment. Would it be worth it to try to attack him right now and throw him off? No, probably not. That gun was just too dangerous. The man was just too dangerous. Fear quivered all through her.

And then she heard the motorcycle. Looking up, she saw Marc coming down the trail. Her heart leaped up and she glanced at Carl. He'd seen Marc too, and he raised his arm, aiming the gun at him.

"No!" she cried, throwing herself at his arm and knocking the gun out of his hand. At the same time, the golf cart hit loose sand and overturned, throwing her out as it tipped, smashing Carl beneath the steel frame. Marc arrived, stopping the motorcycle in a spray of sand and running toward them.

And she went out like a light.

* * *

She woke up on the couch with a blanket over her. She tested all her limbs. She seemed to be okay, except for a wicked headache. As she sat up, Lyla came into the room.

"Hey there, Torie," she said. "What a lot of excitement. I can't tell if you were the gun moll, the damsel in distress or the hero of this whole story."

"What whole story?" she asked, blinking and wishing her head would stop throbbing.

"I guess you did sleep through part of it, didn't you? Well, it seems Carl was not only not your husband, he was a complete crook. You helped Marc catch him. The cops have come and taken him away."

"Oh. Is Marc okay?"

She shrugged. "He looks fine to me. He went with Carl and the police to take care of the paperwork." She sighed. "But I'm leaving myself. Now that the Texan is buying the place, there's no reason for me to stick around."

Torie winced. "Where are you going?"

"Down to Los Angeles. Home."

Torie took a deep breath. More than anything, she wanted to go home. "Can I ride along with you?" she asked. "If Carl's in jail, I guess he won't be driving me."

Lyla laughed. "Sure thing, honey. I'll be glad for the company. But I want to get going in about ten minutes. Think you can make that?"

"Sure." Torie rose from the couch, only wobbling a little bit. "Just give me time to get my suitcase together. I'll meet you out at your car."

She went up the stairs carefully, then went into her room and pulled her suitcase out from under the bed. Reaching in, she drew out the bag of gold coins and looked at it. Then she hurried down the hallway and placed the gold on Marc's bed. Pulling out a pen and a piece of paper, she wrote him a note.

"I think this belongs to you. I found it with my mother's things when I had to move her to a nursing home. This was why I was afraid maybe my father had done something with the treasure after all. I had to come and find out the truth. Now I know that he didn't do it. But I still don't know why he had this bag of gold doubloons. So I'm giving it back."

And that was that. She threw her clothes into her case and headed for the parking area.

"Good bye, Shangri-La," she whispered, looking back at the house. She was surprised to note she didn't have tears in her eyes. "Good bye, Marc. Good bye dream."

And she headed home.

It was almost a week later and she hadn't heard a word from anyone at Shangri-La. She had heard from the police and she'd given a statement about what had happened with Carl. They'd told her she might have to testify. That wasn't a pleasant prospect.

But nothing from Marc. With every day that passed, her hopes grew dimmer, and she was actually getting a bit angry as well. After all, he could at least tell her what his father had written in the journal. She knew he was annoyed with her, but he could at least do that. Still, a part of her wasn't surprised. She'd known from the beginning that a relationship between her and Marc wasn't in the cards. She'd never thought of herself as the Cinderella type.

The bruises on her neck were still visible, but her ankle was doing fine. She'd gone to see her mother and had tried to explain to her that she had found evidence that her father was innocent of everything, but her mother didn't seem to understand what she was talking about. The visit was frustrating, because actually, she didn't have any proof to show her.

And there was still the mystery of the bag of gold. Why hadn't she heard anything from Marc? Maybe he'd given up as well. Now that the Texan was buying the estate, what was there for him to stick around for? He'd probably gone back to wherever it was he'd been over the last year since he got out of the Navy. It was so annoying that she didn't even know that about him. She hardly knew anything, and here she'd thought she might be building a bond between them. She'd been living in a fantasy.

It was Friday. She'd promised her mother she would take her out for ice cream. She pulled up in front of the home and walked to her mother's room with a heavy heart. She'd been so full of hope when she'd left the week before for Shangri-La. And she had nothing to show for it.

As she drew near, she could tell there was someone in the room with her mother. That was strange. The women in the home didn't do much visiting. Who could it be?

"Hi, Mom," she called as she came into the little room. She turned the corner and there was Marc, sitting beside her mother's chair, holding her hand. She stared at him, then looked at her mother. Her eyes were bright and her cheeks were pink. She looked almost like her old self.

"Hi, Torie," Marc said, as though they'd just seen each other somewhere in the last day or so. "I was just telling your mother how good it was to see you again. It was so good, in fact, that I decided I ought to come down and see her, too. Renewing old connections and all that."

Torie sank into a chair and stared at him. "Hi," she said weakly. She was grinning like a loon and blushing like a rose. She could feel it. The smile in his eyes sent her heart soaring.

It was okay. He didn't hate her. Tears welled in her eyes.

"Hey," he said, setting aside her mother's hand and reaching for hers. "Are you okay?"

"I'm fine," she said, embarrassed at how choked her voice sounded. "I'm just…oh, Marc!" Tears were spilling down her face and she was beginning to sob.

He rose and pulled her to her feet, holding her tightly and rocking her gently. "Torie, Torie, didn't you know I'd come and get you as soon as I could?"

"No," she said wetly. "I didn't know that at all."

He turned and smiled at her mother. "Excuse us, Mrs. Sands," he said. "Torie's been through a lot this last week and I've got to take care of her."

"You just go ahead, dear," the woman said, nodding approvingly. "I love her, too."

"Mother!" She hadn't heard that many words from her mother in years. Marc truly knew how to work miracles. She melted in his arms and cried until the tears stopped coming, and then he kissed her face and they all went for ice cream.

Sitting in the little ice cream parlor, he explained a lot to her. And later, when they took her mother back to the home and then went to Torie's apartment and sat on the couch together, he told her more.

"I found that letter my father wrote me shortly before he died," he said. "Now that I know what he was talking about, it was very clear he wanted to let me know about the writings in the journal without letting anyone else—such as Marge—know he'd told me where to look for it."

"So the journal was the key, just as I thought."

"You were right. Your father left it behind,

and my father found it in the attic of your house. He realized there was no way he could hide the truth any longer. He'd done your father a terrible injustice and he felt it deeply. And yet, he wasn't strong enough to make Marge pay for what she'd done."

"And what had she done exactly?"

"From the beginning, she was looking for ways to get some funds together. She wanted to travel, wanted to renovate the house, wanted to have lavish parties. And my father was rapidly going broke. So she hatched a scheme to hide the Don Carlos Treasure in the caves and claim the insurance on it."

"That weekend when everyone was gone."

"Yes. She came back and took the treasure and hid it, then left and pretended she'd been gone the whole time, too."

"Then when the insurance investigators began to suspect as much…."

"She accused your father of having done it. There was never any proof, and when the investigators found the treasure in the cave, the whole thing fell apart on her."

"So your father felt guilty that he'd fired my father and acted like he might be the one who'd done it."

"Right." Marc shook his head. "And once

he couldn't hide the truth any longer, he couldn't live with the guilt."

She frowned speculatively. "So he decided to take the treasure down to the bottom of the sea with him."

"Yes."

"Wow." She made a face. "So sad." Then she had another thought. "And yet, doubloons started appearing all over the place."

"Yes." He moved restlessly. "That's what puzzled me, because I knew my father wouldn't lie. If he said he was going to take the treasure down, he took it down."

"And where did our little bag of gold come from? Finding it made me so scared that my father might have been involved after all."

"He wrote about that in your father's journal. He brought it to your mother, hoping to help her after all she'd been through. He seems to have presented most of the people who used to work for us with at least a few of the coins. Sort of settling scores before he took his life."

Torie shook her head, truly bewildered. "But how…?"

"I'm getting to that. Here's the good part. The Don Carlos Treasure is safely at the bottom of the sea. But there's more gold in the caves. Lots of it." He said it slowly so it would sink in, then grinned at her. "A pirate's treasure trove of it. And my father's writings tell how to get to it."

"Oh." The entire concept of more gold took some getting used to.

"Even after reading his instructions, I wasn't sure if it wasn't just a fantasy of his. I had to work hard out there in the caves. It involved taking apart a whole ledge and getting to the space behind it." He smiled at her. "But I've got it now. And I've used it."

She gazed at him blankly. "What do you mean?"

"I outbid the Texan. I'm buying Shangri-La."

She gasped. "No!"

"Yes. Marge and Shayla are already headed to the Bahamas. I promised not to have her prosecuted for some of the things she's done if she would leave quietly. And she agreed."

"Oh, Marc!"

The look he gave her now was melting. "So now we're set."

"We?"

"We," he repeated. "You've always wanted to live at Shangri-La again, haven't you?"

She could hardly breathe. "Of course, but…"

He touched her cheek. "We'll get married on the patio overlooking the caves and the ocean."

"Oh!" Her head was spinning.

"And we'll bring your mother to live in the gatehouse. We'll hire full-time care for her there."

Torie sat and stared at him, studying every nook and cranny of his handsome face. She couldn't believe it. Was this real?

"Come here," he said, smiling at her.

She blinked at him. "Why?"

He touched her cheek again. "I haven't really kissed you yet."

She shook her head very slowly. She was still worried. "You're not supposed to kiss me."

"Why not?"

"Because we're not here for that. We have thinking to do."

He hooked his hand around her neck and began tugging her closer. "Change your plans," he told her earnestly. "Because kissing is definitely going to happen."

She blinked at him. "Really?"

He nodded. "The urge to kiss a beautiful woman is a powerful force. I've held it off as long as I can."

Now she looked truly worried. "Stop teasing me."

"I'm not teasing you. You're the most beautiful woman I've ever known. And you're going to be mine."

She searched his eyes. "Really? You really want me?"

"More to the point, do you really want me?" He smiled. "Don't you want to kiss me?"

She was melting again, and that was letting the joy in. "Marc Huntington, I've wanted to kiss you since I was ten years old."

"Then come here. We've got some time to make up for."

* * * * *

LARGER-PRINT BOOKS!

GET 2 FREE LARGER-PRINT NOVELS PLUS

2 FREE GIFTS!

HARLEQUIN®

Romance

From the Heart, For the Heart

YES! Please send me 2 FREE LARGER-PRINT Harlequin® Romance novels and my 2 FREE gifts (gifts are worth about $10). After receiving them, if I don't wish to receive any more books, I can return the shipping statement marked "cancel." If I don't cancel, I will receive 6 brand-new novels every month and be billed just $4.59 per book in the U.S. or $5.24 per book in Canada. That's a savings of at least 20% off the cover price! It's quite a bargain! Shipping and handling is just 50¢ per book in the U.S. and 75¢ per book in Canada.* I understand that accepting the 2 free books and gifts places me under no obligation to buy anything. I can always return a shipment and cancel at any time. Even if I never buy another book, the two free books and gifts are mine to keep forever.

119/319 HDN FVSK

Name _____ (PLEASE PRINT)

Address _____ Apt. #

City _____ State/Prov. _____ Zip/Postal Code

Signature (if under 18, a parent or guardian must sign)

Mail to the **Harlequin® Reader Service:**
IN U.S.A.: P.O. Box 1867, Buffalo, NY 14240-1867
IN CANADA: P.O. Box 609, Fort Erie, Ontario L2A 5X3
**Are you a current subscriber to Harlequin Romance books
and want to receive the larger-print edition?
Call 1-800-873-8635 or visit www.ReaderService.com.**

* Terms and prices subject to change without notice. Prices do not include applicable taxes. Sales tax applicable in N.Y. Canadian residents will be charged applicable taxes. Offer not valid in Quebec. This offer is limited to one order per household. Not valid for current subscribers to Harlequin Romance Larger-Print books. All orders subject to credit approval. Credit or debit balances in a customer's account(s) may be offset by any other outstanding balance owed by or to the customer. Please allow 4 to 6 weeks for delivery. Offer available while quantities last.

Your Privacy—The Harlequin® Reader Service is committed to protecting your privacy. Our Privacy Policy is available online at www.ReaderService.com or upon request from the Harlequin Reader Service.

We make a portion of our mailing list available to reputable third parties that offer products we believe may interest you. If you prefer that we not exchange your name with third parties, or if you wish to clarify or modify your communication preferences, please visit us at www.ReaderService.com/consumerschoice or write to us at Harlequin Reader Service Preference Service, P.O. Box 9062, Buffalo, NY 14269. Include your complete name and address.

HRLP13

The series you love are now available in

LARGER PRINT!

The books are complete and unabridged—
printed in a larger type size to make it
easier on your eyes.

◆ **HARLEQUIN**®
Romance

From the Heart, For the Heart

◆ **HARLEQUIN**®
MEDICAL™
Pulse-racing romance,
heart-racing medical drama

◆ **HARLEQUIN**®
INTRIGUE®
BREATHTAKING ROMANTIC SUSPENSE

◆ **HARLEQUIN**®
Presents®

Seduction and Passion Guaranteed!

◆ **HARLEQUIN**®
super romance®

Exciting, emotional, unexpected!

Try **LARGER PRINT** today!

Visit: www.ReaderService.com
Call: 1-800-873-8635

◆ **HARLEQUIN**®
™

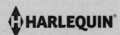
A *Romance* FOR EVERY MOOD™

www.ReaderService.com

HLPDIR13

ReaderService.com

Manage your account online!
- Review your order history
- Manage your payments
- Update your address

*We've designed
the Harlequin® Reader Service
website just for you.*

Enjoy all the features!
- Reader excerpts from any series
- Respond to mailings and
  special monthly offers
- Discover new series available to you
- Browse the Bonus Bucks catalog
- Share your feedback

Visit us at:
ReaderService.com

RS13